BOYS and GIRLS TOGETHER

BOYS
and
GIRLS
TOGETHER

William Saroyan

Barricade Books Inc.
New York

Published by Barricade Books Inc.
150 Fifth Avenue
New York, NY 10011

Printed in the United States of America.

Library of Congress Cataloging-in-Publication Data

Saroyan, William, 1908–1981
Boys and girls together: a novel / William Saroyan.
p.   cm.\ISBN 1-56980-047-2 (pbk)
1. Married people—United States—Fiction. 2. Parent and child—
United States—Fiction. I. Title.
PS3537.A826B6 1995
813'.52—dc20   95-21745
CIP

First printing

Tasol nambawan taim God i wokim ol samting, em i wokim man na meri. Orait.
(Gud Nius Mak i Raitim. St. Mark's Gospel in Neo Melanesian, or Pidgin English.)

That's all number one time God he walk them all same thing, he walk them man and woman. All right.
(Saroyan-American, or Buzzard English.)

But from the beginning of the creation God made them male and female. Verily.
(The Gospel According to Saint Mark, Chapter 10, Verse 6. King James Version, or Chicken English.)

BOYS and GIRLS TOGETHER

CHAPTER
1

They were sitting in the parlor they both hated so much but somehow liked, too, and there wasn't a thing doing. They were married, there were the two kids out of it, the boy first and then the girl, and now the kids were asleep at last, or at any rate in bed. They were trying to think what to say so they wouldn't be just sitting there, but there wasn't really anything to say unless they fell into dirty talk, which they frequently did.

"I saw Charley's wife when I took the girl walking," the woman said. "Who did you see when you took the boy walking?"

"I didn't see anybody. Who's Charley's wife?"

"Ellen. Didn't you see a girl?"

"I saw a girl standing on the corner waiting for a streetcar."

"Would she be as good as me?"

"Once or twice maybe she would, but I don't want a fight."

"If you don't want a fight, why do you look at every girl you see and wonder how she'd be?"

"It's a habit."

"She was a dog and you know it."

"She didn't seem a dog when I saw her. She seemed clean and hopeful, but later on she could easily become a dog."

"Do you mean that's what I've become?"

"I don't know what you've become."

"Oh yes you do."

"What have you become?"

"I've become a good wife, and a good mother, and damned tired of it, too."

"It's what you wanted. It *is* tiring, though, I suppose. Now, if you'd take a bath and get yourself relaxed once the kids are out of the way every night, maybe it wouldn't be so tiring."

"I'm too tired to take a bath. I'm so hungry I can't stand the thought of eating the things we know how to cook."

"If you'd take a bath, you'd be able to stand the thought."

"No, I'd just want to put on my best clothes and go out and have two or three drinks and a real supper."

"Well, we can't do that, but if you'll take a bath and put on your best clothes, I'll open two cans of chili. I'll have everything ready when you're ready and we'll have two or three Scotches apiece before we eat the chili."

"After we eat, what'll we do?"

"Let's eat first."

"Do you think we'll know then?"

"We *ought* to. Go ahead, take your bath and take your time."

"I'll put on some perfume, too."

"I like the way you smell after a bath without perfume, but maybe you don't, so put some on if it makes you happy. I like the smell of clean skin that's breathing."

"I won't put any on, then. Don't you smell the soap?"

"I like to smell the soap."

"If the boy gets out of bed, spank him."

"O.K."

He went to the woman and hugged her. She smelled tired and dirty and frightened. Her skin was suffocating with dirty sweat, and the expensive perfume she'd used that afternoon made the smell worse.

4

"Don't kiss me now. Don't spoil it in case we think of something after the chili."

"Go bathe."

The wife went to the bathroom and the husband heard her singing softly, almost happily. When she was in the tub the door of the bedroom opened and the boy came out in his bare feet.

"Where's Mama?"

"She's bathing."

"I want to bathe with her."

"You can't. Now, go right back and get into your bed."

"I want a drink of water first."

The father let the water run out of the kitchen faucet until it was fresh and cool, and then he handed the son a glass of water and the five-year-old drank it all and handed back the empty glass. The water always satisfied him. He always had the same expression of satisfaction on his face when he handed back the glass. It was something like a wink.

"Why don't you take a bath, too?"

"I will."

"I mean with Mama."

"O.K. Get back in your bed."

"Good night."

"O.K."

He saw the boy back into his bed, still almost winking with satisfaction. He went across the room to have another look at his two-and-a-half-year-old daughter's bare body, with the bottom up in the air. Her little body was just about the prettiest thing he had ever seen. He went out of the room wondering what it was she was always thinking about in her sleep.

He knew what it was he was always thinking about in *his* sleep because he'd had thirty-nine years to find out.

He went to the kitchen, got out the two cans of chili and began to read the label on one of them for instructions, and then decided to have one drink before the body of the girl in the bathtub came out to have one with him.

CHAPTER
2

After the drink he went to the bathroom door and said, "Don't misunderstand this, but I need a bath myself and the boy wanted to know why I didn't bathe with you, but don't get any ideas about it."

"Did you spank him?"

"Hell no. He wanted a drink of water. He's fast asleep again. But forget it. I'll take a shower after the chili. I don't want to spoil your bath."

"No. The door's open. Come on in."

He went in and saw that she was already looking cleaner and more hopeful, and the body sat there almost as if it were in a boy's dream.

"I'll brush my teeth, and shave."

"Will you scrub my back? I can't reach it."

"Sure, but don't hurry your bath. Don't make another job out of it. After you're all relaxed and clean, get into the shower and cool off."

"I don't want a shower, *too*."

"The shower gets all the sweat and dirt and soap off your skin, and then when you make the water cold it tightens your skin all over and brings out all of its color. You should always take a shower after a bath."

6

"O.K., then. Do you think I'm too fat?"

"You're not fat at all."

"Oh yes I am." She stood suddenly. "Here, and all in here, and how about up here?"

"That isn't fat. That's woman. Another thing entirely."

"Was she as woman as I am?"

"Who?"

"The girl you saw waiting for the streetcar that you think was so clean and hopeful."

"Oh." He rinsed the toothpaste suds out of his mouth. "No, she wasn't."

"There you go again being a crook, just because you're beginning to think of something to do after the chili."

"No, she was kind of skinny."

"I know you're trying to con me just because you've hit on some sort of idea for after the chili, because every time you hit on an idea something happens to your voice."

"What happens?"

"It gets horny. In spite of everything you do to keep it from getting horny, it gets horny, because once you get an idea you're a dead Indian. I could make an awful fool of you any time I felt like it if I wanted to go to the trouble of taking off my clothes."

"You'd make an awful fool of yourself, too."

"I don't mean when we're with people or anything like that. I mean when we're alone. I found out about that before we were married when we went swimming in the ocean naked at night and the water was so cold you'd think it would freeze a man's balls off. I thought it was because we weren't married yet, and that's why I made all that fuss a couple of months after we were married about going swimming that way again. I wanted to find out."

"A couple of months after we were married you were pregnant, and it wasn't supposed to be good for you to go swimming that way."

"Doctors don't know too much about things like that. Anyhow, it didn't do me any harm, and I found out that it wasn't

7

because we hadn't been married. It was because you go a little nuts when you see a girl's body. You can be freezing and still go a little nuts. And it's not because the body's mine. It could be any girl's."

"Maybe it *couldn't*." He began to shave.

"Not only that. Any *woman's* body, any woman at all, not just the body of a twenty-year-old girl, but the body of a thirty- or forty- or fifty-year-old woman. I'll bet you've had women who've been *more* than fifty."

"Maybe I have."

"*Old* bags. Any kind of woman at all."

"Except intellectuals."

"You've had *them,* too. You know damn well you have."

"Some. But I didn't like it."

"You've had *plenty* of them. What about that woman who's so active in the Communist Party? Who lies down with all her clothes on to anybody at all, and opens up and takes away the clothes that are in the way, while her husband's handing drinks around to the guests downstairs? Before we were married I saw you go upstairs with her, and when you came downstairs ten minutes later I knew you'd had her because she was so sweet to me, and superior, and because you were so friendly to her husband. I suppose you didn't have *her* that time?"

"So what?"

"And she didn't even take off her clothes. She *couldn't* have. There wasn't time."

"There was."

"She *couldn't* have taken off her clothes. What kind of a woman is a woman like that? How could she take off her clothes and do it and be back downstairs in ten minutes?"

"Eleven or twelve minutes."

"Well, what kind of a woman is *that?* What did you *say* to her?"

"We talked about Russia."

"You *didn't*."

"She told me about the time she was in Kiev and I told her about the time I was in Kharkov."

"And then, you were in *her*."

"Well, yes, but she talked about Kiev as if she had just won the hundred-yard dash."

"And you talked the same as ever, the way you always do. Is it that way with other men?"

"*You* tell me."

"You know I've never been with anybody in this whole world except you. You know I didn't know my ass from a hole in the ground when I met you. Is it that way with *her* husband, or does he squeal and squeak the way a woman sometimes wants to do? I've always been ashamed to, because I've been afraid you'd laugh at me."

"You can squeal and squeak any time you feel like it. I won't laugh at you. I guess every man does everything his own way, and maybe some men squeal and squeak but I wouldn't know about her husband."

"How would you feel if I took a man at a cocktail party upstairs and did that?"

"You're not an intellectual."

"I can talk about Kiev as well as she can. How would you feel if I did that?"

"I'd stop you."

"Why? Why would you stop me?"

"Because I know it would make you unhappy."

"That's what *you* think. I'm going to do it, too." She was finished soaping her body, and now she sat back in the water. "Will you scrub my back?"

CHAPTER
3

He began to scrub, and she said, "Do you want to get in with me and bathe, too?"

He scrubbed hard and saw the smooth pink skin turn red. "I won't spoil your bath, and I've got to get the chili and drinks."

"You're being a crook again and you know it. Something I said has stopped you from being horny and you're trying to pretend you want to be nice."

"Don't be silly. I'll take a shower after we eat. You finish your bath and take a shower and I'll have everything all set. I just wanted to brush my teeth and shave."

"You wanted to look at me, because I'm a girl's body."

"I like to look at you all right. Shall I scrub some more?"

"Scrub a lot. Scrub all the way down. Scrub anywhere you like." She stretched out in the water and waited to see where he would scrub. He scrubbed where she hoped he would, and she watched his face to see if she could guess what he was thinking, and then she said, "When I was in Kiev there was a member of the Party there who asked if he might show me the Theatre for Children Orphaned by the Revolution."

"Oh?"

"He was one of the most brilliant men I ever met. He had

10

black hair, black skin, and a very black thing, too, as I later happened to notice."

"Oh?"

"We went straight to the Theatre, but of course it was empty because it was one o'clock in the morning. He was so brilliant. He lived for the Party. He lived for it night and day. We had the party on the stage all over the floor and furniture of a set that was supposed to be a Russian millionaire's parlor before the revolution."

"O.K. Now get the hell into the shower and take your time about drying and combing your hair. Comb it straight down, long, and don't pile it up on top of your head on the theory that it makes you look seductive."

"Don't you want to hear any more about Kiev?"

"You're not an intellectual."

"Well, what did *she* say that was so much better than what I said?"

"She emphasized the wonderful new life that was going to come out of Communism. She didn't mention any man with black hair and black skin. I'll go fix the chili and get the drinks."

"Don't you want to tell me something about Kharkov?"

"It was full of bores, the same as San Francisco, or any other place. Get into the shower and turn on the cold water."

"Do we *have* to have chili?"

"Why?"

"I'm not hungry any more. Are you?"

"Not if you're not."

"Let's just drink."

"O.K. Take your time."

"You take yours, too."

He went out and fixed himself another drink. He was drinking when the doorbell rang, and he thought, "If this is some stupid friend, I'm just going to have to tell him I'm working and can't stop just now."

He opened the door and it was Charley Flesch and his wife, Ellen.

11

"Hi," Ellen said. "Daisy asked us over after dinner. We got a sitter for the kids after phoning about a dozen of them and we came right over."

They were both in now and he was showing Charley where to put his hat and coat. He'd told her never to ask people over without letting him know, so now here they were.

"How've you been? Sit down and I'll bring you a drink. Daisy's had a rough day and she's having a shower. Scotch?"

"Scotch is just what I've been dreaming about all day," Charley said. "Is there enough for a stiff one to start and a couple of mild ones to keep it going?"

"There's plenty. Ellen?"

"The same, thanks, Dick, but let me help with the glasses or something."

"No, just sit still. I'll only be a minute. Turn on the radio if you like, or both of you come along and pour them the way you like them."

"Yes," Charley said, "that's the thing to do."

At the bathroom door he called out cheerfully, "Oh, Daisy, can you hear me?"

The shower water was going but he heard it stop, and then he heard her say, "Do you want to tell me something about Kharkov?"

"No. It's Ellen and Charley. I'm getting us all a drink. Hurry along and join us."

Her silence was too long, but maybe Ellen and Charley didn't notice. She was remembering that she had as a matter of fact asked Ellen to come over after dinner and she had forgotten all about it, so now here they were all set to start drinking and they wouldn't be gone until after midnight.

"Hi, Ellen, hi, Charley," she called out suddenly. "I'll be out in a minute."

CHAPTER
4

"Well, how's the writing game?" Charley Flesch said.

"I'm practically retired. You know how it is with the women who are supposed to look after your kids. First, they're wonderful, and then all of a sudden they're a bigger problem than the kids, a bigger problem than the bride, a bigger problem than marriage itself. You know you ought to fire her, but you don't do it, because you don't want to have to do all that work yourself, but the bride keeps telling you every night in bed what a dog the woman is with the kids, how she pretends to love them but actually hates them, how she keeps trying to teach them her idea of manners, how she is forever comparing them with her own grandchildren who are so much more intelligent and handsome and well-behaved, and how she secretly slaps them because the little boy himself told her so, and then at last you give her a bonus and send her away, and that's what happened three months ago. So naturally I've been out of touch with the writing game. How are things in the barber game?"

"You'd think it was the same thing," Ellen said. "You'd think being a barber and being a writer was the same kind of thing."

"Shut up, please," Charley said cheerfully. "I'm drinking

and I'm happy. I know being a barber isn't the same as being a writer, but neither is being anything else. Am I right, Dick? And since nothing is the same as being a writer, it's just as much fun for a writer to compare notes with a barber as it is with anybody else."

"Except maybe with another writer," Ellen said.

"No," Charley said. "Dick don't like talking to other writers. How do I know? I read it in one of his books, the one you gave us for Christmas, Dick. It's right in there some place. You come right out in there some place and say you don't give a shit for writers. Pardon the expression, Ellen."

"You just shut up or talk clean," Ellen said. "Just don't get too smart just because Dick's not like other famous people."

"Shut up, for God's sake," Charley said. "I was only quoting Dick. Am I right, Dick? I never knew writers used words like the words barbers use, but I know different now. I know at least one writer who uses the words barbers use. Dick is the one who said he don't give a shit for writers. It wasn't me."

"Now you just stop it," Ellen said. "It's one thing for Dick to write something and another for you to say it. He probably meant something you don't understand."

"What did you mean, Dick?" Charley said.

The man laughed, although he wished to God Daisy hadn't gone to work and asked them over tonight, because here they were, like two earnest and comic characters in a bad movie, each of them a little too impressed by his name because it was so often in the papers and because a name in the papers signified so much to them, and he said, "To tell you the truth, you're *both* right about that crack I made, but let's talk about something that makes sense. Ellen, tell me about Ronald and Greta."

"Oh, they're the same as ever. God, the things they say, the things they do. Greta gets up from her nap this afternoon and says, 'Mama, why do girls have those?' You know what she means—up here—so I been reading them damn books that tell you all about everything and I figure I've got to tell her the real reason, but I just can't remember it, so finally I tell her it's so you can tell girls from boys, but she comes right back and says she's a girl and not a boy, so where's hers and she starts squawking because she hasn't got hers. Them damn books."

"You could tell her girls have them because they're pretty and because boys like girls to have them, couldn't you?" Charley said.

"All right, wise guy, so if I said that, wouldn't she still come right back and say she wanted hers *now*? What good would it do to say that? That doesn't make her any happier than what I told her."

"Ah, you could have told her girls have them because boys like to see them and take hold of them, couldn't you?"

"You just shut up. And don't stare at mine like a damn calf."

"You *think* they're yours," Charley said. "They're mine, little woman. You just carry them around for me. And all the rest of it, too. Am I right, Dick? Just because I run a four-chair barbershop that's all paid for don't necessarily mean I don't have a kind of half-assed philosophy of my own, you know. I gave a lot of time to thinking once I got out of high school, and I came to a lot of pretty good conclusions. I may be wrong in a few of them, but only a little wrong. I didn't stand on my feet cutting hair for fifteen years for nothing, you know. I learned a thing or two on my own without any help from any books, and what did it finally boil down to? Them two things." Charley roared with laughter. "Them two, and the two on the other side, and the depot out front, and all of it together in one small package that gets bigger and bigger the more you try to think it isn't anything. Sure you get kids out of it, and headaches, and bills to pay, but so what? It's worth it."

Now Ellen burst out laughing because she was so thrilled about the things her husband had said and the impression he had made on the writer, and because he never seemed to come alive so boldly as when they were visiting the writer and his wife.

"You just shut up," she giggled.

"You know you love it," Charley said, controlling his voice so that he would not be giggling, too. "You know damn well what it does to you. The thing Gable used to do to you when you were a little girl going to the movies with a half-dozen other little girls."

"Hey!" Daisy called from the bathroom. "Wait for me. I want to get in on the fun, too."

"Don't worry," the writer called back to her. "There's plenty more where that came from. Am I right, Charley?"

"*Pa*lenty," the barber said.

"I'll go get you another." He took the barber's empty glass.

"Small, though. At least *smaller*. I start out fast but I can't keep it up for long."

The man went to get the barber another drink.

CHAPTER
5

By the time Daisy came out of the bedroom, where she had
her fixing-up table and her junk, the barber and his wife were
singing a favorite song of the barber's, the one about Maggie,
when she had been young, and the old man who'd got her for
his wife had been young, too. Daisy was really fixed up, she
wasn't going to let the arrival of the barber and his wife spoil
anything for her, not even if they didn't have sense enough
to get up and go until one or two in the morning. She was
fixed up and knew it, and the man knew it, and the barber
had to stop singing a second to whistle his admiration, but he
went right on singing after the whistle. Daisy and Ellen met
one another as girls like to do and touched cheeks, and then
Daisy said, "Well, what about *me*, where's my drink?"

"Go and get it," the man said because he wanted her to
know he knew all about how fixed up she was. He wanted
her not to get too important because she knew how good it
made him feel to see her so fresh and young and pretty and
eager about the sport that was always there to be had between
them.

She gave him the limpid look that always meant the same
thing, that always meant all you got to do is tell me what to
do and I'll do it, just tell me and it will be done, and then

17

when she knew the man had got the message she lifted her head in an imitation of aloofness and went off for her drink while the singing went right on. When she didn't come back after she had had time enough to fix two drinks he knew what she was up to, so he went after her while the barber and his wife asked one another what else to sing. And there she was as he knew she'd be, her back to him but knowing he'd be there in a moment, the empty glass before her and everything ready to be mixed but nothing mixed. He went to her and took her in his arms and held her very tight, then moved his hands all over, slowly and softly. She lowered the zipper so he'd not have cloth in the way, but he lifted it and said, "Don't be rude to your guests." And then very loudly so that they'd hear him he said, "Never mind sneaking an extra drink in here, Daisy. Get right back where you belong."

"Yeah," Ellen said, "we've only had three each, and Charley's drooling already."

"And you know what I'm drooling *for,* too," Charley said.

The man fixed his wife a big one and twisted her head around and held his open mouth to hers after she'd had a sip and the tongue jumped up and tried to take up all the space, but he turned her around and they went back into the living room together to find the barber and his wife kissing.

"Well," the barber said getting up, "we'll be going home now, if you know what I mean."

"Ah, sit down," Ellen said.

"O.K., you asked for it," the barber said to his wife, "but you know damn well one more drink and when I hit the bed it will be dreamland for me and nothing else."

"Won't be the first time," Ellen said as if she were saying the right thing.

"You're darn tootin' it won't," the barber said proudly. "Well, Daisy, I guess you know you look like something bad little boys dream about. I guess you know that. Am I right, Dick?"

"Any woman can do it if you'll give her a tub and some

hot water to bathe in and enough time to believe she's got it, and a few kind words."

"Yeah," the barber said, "that's all they really need, a little soap and a few kind words. I get a kick out of the way I can always get the little woman to think she's got anything Betty Grable ever had and a few little things she ain't got."

"It happens," Ellen said, "I happen to admire Betty Grable and have no delusions about myself. I happen to know I'm younger than Miss Grable and I also happen to know I went further in school than she did."

"What else do you happen to know?" the barber said. "She knows a few other things, too. I think it has to do with the kind of people she comes from."

"My family wasn't rich," Ellen said, "but they kept out of jail."

"They were pretty religious, too, weren't they?" Charley said. "Hell, tell Dick and Daisy how religious they were."

"They went to church every Sunday," Ellen said, "and I happen to think it did them no harm."

"No, no," Charley said. "Tell them how they were in the Presbyterian Church for maybe thirty or forty years."

"Maybe more," Ellen said. "Anyhow, they were always good Presbyterians."

"What she's trying to say," Charley said, "is that they were better than my people, who were Lutherans."

"No," Ellen said earnestly, "that's not what I'm trying to say at all. It happens that I happen to think rather highly of the Lutherans, although to be perfectly honest I don't know what they believe."

"They believe having kids is the duty of every married couple," Charley said, "but I guess you know why they believe it."

"They believe it because it's in the Bible," Ellen said.

"The hell they do," Charley said. "They believe it because they know what you've got to do to get kids."

"Say," Ellen said suddenly, "is he laughing at me or something? Is he, Daisy?"

19

"You and your religion," Charley said. "I'm your religion and you ain't nothing without me. Absolutely nothing."

"I suppose you *are* something without me," Ellen said.

"Just a barber without you," the husband confessed, "but with you—well, you and me know, don't we, chicken?"

"Yeah, we know all right," Ellen said, trying to get sober and trying to get Dick and Daisy into the fun. "What we know you could put in a nutshell and have room left over for the Encyclopaedia Britannica or something."

The telephone bell rang and the man answered it. He had to stay on the line almost ten minutes. During that time Daisy and Ellen went into the kitchen together to get fresh drinks for themselves and another for Charley, even though Ellen had been warned he'd fall asleep the minute he got home, and Charley wandered around in the living room talking to himself and trying not to hear what the man was saying on the telephone, but of course he knew the call was from New York and the talk was about a play. They were back in the living room when he finished talking.

"Cooper. He thinks he's got a producer for the play. An *old* play, Ellen. Something I had to drag out of the trunk because Daisy thinks we're too poor. Does Ellen make you do things like that, too, Charley?"

"Does she? First I had two chairs and I was making a good living, but she said that wasn't enough, so I put in another, but that wasn't enough either, so I put in a fourth one. Well, do you think that satisfied her? Hell no. Now she wants me to rent the empty store next door, break down the wall and make it an eight-chair shop. So what am I going to do? I'm going to make it an eight-chair shop. I'll say she gooses me. She gooses me all the time. Is it a good play?"

"I think it stinks, but Daisy doesn't care about that. She's crazy about money, that's all."

"And boys," Daisy said.

"She doesn't care if I ruin my name, she just wants to see more money."

"What's the name of the play?" the barber said.

20

"It used to be called *The Idiots,* but Daisy said nobody would go to a play with a name like that, so I changed it to *Free for All.*"

"That's a pretty good name for a play, too," the barber said. He was pretty well gone now, but he was trying not to be, and his talk was slowing down and getting serious and a little self-conscious. He seemed in fact to be a little unhappy in a kind of vague way, the way it is when the top of the alcohol happiness has been reached and a man knows he's sinking fast, sinking into the lonely sleep of a small boy who expects a lot some day and is pretty sure he expects too much.

"Free for All," the barber said. "What's it about, a fight?"

"Well, yes, in a way."

"A writer don't like to tell what everything he writes is about," Ellen said.

"Don't be silly," Daisy said to Ellen. "Dick loves to talk about his writing. He drives me crazy talking about it all the time, morning, noon and night."

"Well, anyhow," the barber said, "is it a kind of brawl in a saloon or something like that, a free-for-all, the way we used to have them sometimes when I was in the Army and we were in a little town and the Navy came in and tried to take over. Is it something like that?"

"Yes, it is."

"Jesus," the barber said, "one time there I took a hell of a beating. I thought I was going to get killed in the saloon instead of in the war, but I didn't feel so bad because I knew they'd say I died a hero and Ellen would get the insurance and decoration."

The man half listened to his wife and the barber's wife go after themes of their own, kids and schools and nurses and baby sitters and groceries and all the rest of it, and then he and Charley went after fresh drinks and stayed in the kitchen until Charley began to nearly fall over now and then, and then the barber said, "Jesus, Dick, I wish to Christ I knew how to write because the God-damn stuff I know would make a hell of a book. I wish to God I'd taken it up instead of barbering, not that I ain't doing all right. I own the shop, I've paid for the house, Ellen's got clothes from Magnin's and the other good shops—she's got something from Ransohoff's that cost a hundred bucks—and I've got a few bucks put away for the kids, for college, I mean, but hell, if I'd taken it up I wouldn't have to hang around a barbershop all day talking to a lot of bums. I'd be in my damn studio writing books."

The man moved back into the living room and Charley said, "Come on, chicken, bedtime for the old man now. And listen, Daisy, it sure was nice of you and Dick to ask us over. I'll have a hangover in the morning, but it was worth it. I haven't had so many laughs in a long time. Will you come over to our place Saturday night?"

"Sure," the man's wife said the way she always did.

"We'll try," the man said. "Daisy'll phone Ellen Friday afternoon about it."

"O.K.," the barber said. "I'll have a new bottle of black label to open."

After a minute they were gone, and the man said, "I wish you wouldn't invite everybody you run into to come here quick—real quick, the way it was tonight—you could have said day after tomorrow, couldn't you, so I could get out of it?"

"I thought you had fun," the woman said.

"I did, but I'm starved and drunk and bored to death and the night's shot to hell, and there you are looking real crazy."

The woman didn't say anything. She put out all the lights except a little one and then zipped her clothing straight off and laughed, and the man began to take off his.

"Look at the fool I'm making of you," the woman said, holding her arms out and dancing slowly. "Shall I stop?"

"Sure."

"What a crook."

"No, I mean it."

"O.K."

The man looked at her a moment, and then he said, "I stink. I'll get in the shower. You go right on dancing."

"Don't be funny."

"O.K., then, get some chili."

"Chili? Are you crazy?"

"Hell no, starved. I've got to get something besides Scotch inside my gut."

"You mean you want to *eat?*"

"Hell yes."

"You want me to put my clothes back on?"

"Who said anything about that?" Out of his clothes now, he lifted himself into shape, lifted the bulge at the belly, so it wouldn't be so noticeable. The woman looked at him and laughed.

"Look at you," she said, pointing and laughing. "Just look at you, and you want to eat. God, are other men like that, too?"

"Just get me some chili. And dance a little more before I go."

The woman danced saying, "You dog, you just won't *ever* get completely helpless, will you? The way other men do?"

"No," the man said. "I'll be out in a minute. There's a box of crackers somewhere, too."

He went to the bathroom and the woman went to work in the kitchen.

CHAPTER
6

He felt good in the shower and was full of smiling inside because she was something at that, she was as nearly something as any woman he had ever known and probably more nearly something than any wife he could think of, anybody's wife he could think of, even though she was a lot that was a pain in the ass if the kids weren't asleep and the day wasn't over and she hadn't had a bath and he hadn't had a couple to drink and the going was another kind of going, she was a lot like that, too much like that if she ever wanted to know the truth about herself, a nagging nuisance until it was a time like this, and the most astonishing kind of crook he could imagine, and she could get so ugly he'd have to either hit her or get out of the house and walk somewhere in a hurry, talking to himself, hating her, hating her stupid mother, her stupid grandmother, her stupid father and her stupid grandfather. If it weren't for the kids, he'd have thrown her out long ago, he'd have told her to hit the road, which was what she had coming, get the hell back to where she came from and not bother him any more, just because she had it, just because it was good. If it weren't for the way the little girl's bare bottom made his soul rejoice every time he saw it sticking up in her crib and the way her thoughtful face made him love

her even more than he loved the boy, he'd have told her to
get up and go back where she belonged, he would have told
her to marry somebody she deserved, not him, because she
just didn't go with him, she just couldn't, he had to carry her
every minute, he had to give her lies and her ugliness all sorts
of values they weren't entitled to, he had to do it all the time,
just because she happened to have it good, and they happened
to have the two kids. If it weren't for the way the boy winked
with his expression when he was satisfied and liked the ab-
surdity of being alive, didn't know any better because Papa
was there to look after him, and Mama was there to smell
good to him and feel good to him when she hugged him,
and his little sister was there for him to be nice to the way
Papa was nice to Mama, tolerating her ignorance and her
selfishness and her bad manners, letting her be his little
bride, letting her nag at him for things that were his, letting
her put her arms around him when she was sorry about
something, letting her tell him she was sorry, if it wasn't for
the way the boy liked the whole idea of all of them being together and fighting it out, he would have told her to hit the
road and go out and make a name for herself walking the
streets or peddling it out of a call house or getting famous in
the movies by spreading it around among the fat old men
who help a girl along. It would be another story if it weren't
for the kids, but she was something at that, she was very nearly
something just the same, and now he was full of smiling inside
about her, even though he hadn't forgotten the truth about
her, either, or about himself, either, the lousy truth about
both of them.

The table was all set and the chili was in the bowls. He'd
bought the bowls especially for chili because he'd always liked
it, and you could get it out of a can any time you liked, but
it ought to be eaten out of a bowl, the way it had been long
ago when he used to step into a chili joint and put away a
bowl, crumbling half a dozen crackers into the red greasy
juice. He had eaten it regularly from the time he'd been
thirteen to the time he'd been eighteen, and he'd eaten it

after that as often as he could find a place where they had it, and then he missed it for years, but all of a sudden it began to come in cans, and he had it back, beans and pieces of slobbery meat and the thick red greasy juice.

She was covered up now in a peach-colored robe that was made so you could see through it, and she looked sad, like a little girl who's thinking sad thoughts, something about how strange life is, so he knew what was coming.

"Do you love me, Dick?"

That was what was coming.

He began to eat the chili.

"There's two kids inside there sleeping. We've been together six years. We were together a year before that, before we got married."

"Yes, but do you love me?"

"O.K. I love you."

"You crook."

"That's right."

"Well, why *don't* you love me?"

"We've talked about this just about every night for seven years. I've told you all about it. You're welcome to lies if they make you happy. You're welcome to the truth if you insist on having it. Thanks for fixing the chili. You'd better have some."

The woman began to eat. She wasn't acting now, she was as serious as anybody could be, he would like to be as nice as possible, but she was always asking him the questions you have got to try to answer honestly and that meant that even if he tried to be nice she would know he wasn't telling the truth, and she wouldn't like it. She wanted lies to be true, that's all.

"Well, then, why isn't it possible for anybody to really love anybody?" she said.

"I don't know. It's certainly one of the things a man ought to try to get straight. Now, when you ask somebody if he loves you, you make it impossible for him to love you. The lousy question does it. And it's not that somebody *can't* love somebody sometimes. He can. He can really love somebody, but he can't say he loves somebody because somebody asks him if he does? I mean anything he says at that time is either a lie or meaningless."

"*When* do you love me?"

"When you shut up for a while. When it seems to me that something's going on in your head that is quiet and lonely and straight and maybe even lovely. Maybe no such thing is actually going on, but I love you when there is only no evidence that it isn't. I really love you, then. I love you tenderly, then. I almost forget all about the red and raw body you've got that I enjoy so much, and I really love you, then."

"Well, I don't want you to forget the body, either."

"Neither do I want to forget it, but when you shut up and go about fussing with the kids in a nice way and quiet down and think about something besides the things you're always thinking about, then I really love you. And I love you when you bawl. That's the truth. That's the only thing in the world that has ever made me helpless, the way you bawl, because you bawl like all the stupid little girls of the human race bawling. I swear to God it breaks my heart when you bawl. I never saw anybody bawl that way, not even kids, except our own, both of them bawl that way."

"I'm going to bawl all the time. I'm going to bawl right now while I'm eating this awful chili."

"Go ahead. And don't think I don't know you're smart enough to do it any time you feel like it, too, because I do. Even so, even then, the way you bawl breaks my heart and makes me love you, makes me want to protect you, take care of you."

"Well, *that's* something, anyway. Do you want the rest of my chili?"

"You eat it. You've had nothing to eat since lunch. Christ, it's almost two, and the kids are going to start running all over the place at six."

"Ignore them. I've told you to ignore them or spank them and put them back to bed."

"You're so God-damn smart. They can't be ignored. They've got to be washed and dressed and given breakfast and turned loose in the yard, so they can live."

"I don't want any more of it. You finish the rest of mine. I don't know how you can enjoy something so awful so much." She pushed the bowl across the table, and he finished what was in it before he spoke again.

"It's good food. Especially now that it comes in cans. Is there any beer?"

The woman fetched a can of beer from the refrigerator and he slapped her bottom when she moved past him so she'd know he was still thinking about how she had it. She poured beer into a glass and then she said, "It's too late."

"Shut up."

"It really *is* too late. Don't think I don't appreciate your letting me sleep in the morning while you get the kids out into the yard. I just can't get up in the mornings. You need all the sleep you can get."

The man got up and finished the beer and walked into the dark living room.

"Just shut up. And come here."

"No. In the bedroom."

"Why?"

"I've got it all fixed up. It's nice and clean in there."

"O.K."

"Will you tell me about Kharkov?"

"Sure."

"All the time?"

"Sure."

"Every minute of the time. Tell me all about it."

28

CHAPTER
7

When a man is too near his pleasure, he thought, the food and drink of his heart and hide, too near the satisfying of the gross and grand appetite—but there was never a time like this before, an appetite or a feast like this—when that is how it is with a man, then the luck of children is greater, the luck of art less, though work is best, art is best, the insatiable appetite denied is best, or so they say, they say, but whenever she's there with eyes, hair, mouth, moisture, they don't say it.

"I do this for children," he said.

"You dog. I do it for you."

"You do it for you, I do it for me, and to hell with lies."

"Well, it's not my fault I've got to lie."

"Whose fault is it?"

"Johnny's. He started the whole thing."

Maybe it was the sleeping boy's fault at that, because if Johnny hadn't come along, it would have been another story: the hard dark man, dark the day he was born, darker every day, but the skin fair, the eyes bright with light, not bright with color, dark with color, bright with light, with the light that was his mother's own light, the light of the bawling girl, the little girl stamping her feet for love, for the right to belong somewhere specific and not be loose all over the place,

29

the right to mean everything to one man, it was her own fire that put the light in him, it was the light of the bawling girl no longer bawling but thinking, "I made it. I bawled for it and got it."

"Isn't it time to tell me about Kharkov?"

"Kharkov, if you say it right, is like clearing the throat, but there are those who call it Harkov."

"That's nice."

"Yes, it is, because hark is a fair word, as words go in English."

"Hark hark the lark. Do you feel the fluttering of the lark?"

"That I do."

"It's his fault. When he comes in here in the morning spank him. What would I be doing now except for him? You know you can't say you don't love me *now*."

"No, I can't."

CHAPTER
8

They listened to the streetcar banging down the street to the ocean, knowing it had no passengers at that hour of the night, or only one drunk, or an old woman who'd gone across the bay to Berkeley to visit a married daughter, the conductor up front beside the motorman, the two of them talking above the noise of the downhill banging, and smoking cigarettes.

"Shall I stick it up the way the little girl does?"

"Yes, I'd like to see that."

"But don't look until I'm ready, all right?"

"All right."

This is what we do, the man thought, and out of it the earth is peopled.

"Ready."

He turned and saw her stuck up the way the little girl always was when she was asleep, and it was astonishing, it was just like the little girl, the bottom gone west with womanhood, wide and thick and whiter than the little girl's, but the head almost no different at all, the same face, the same thoughtfulness, but now the mother opened her eyes to be both the little girl and the little girl's mother, the eyes limpid, lewd and loving.

"Do you like it?"

31

"Yes."

"Is it as good as ice cream?"

"Better."

"Is it true what they say about the Japanese?"

"That was propaganda to make the soldiers hate them."

"I don't mean the war. I mean the wonderful thoughtfulness of them in such things."

"I knew what you meant."

"Isn't it wonderful of the Japanese to be so thoughtful?"

"Don't you mean experimental?"

"What's that mean?"

"To experiment."

"Well, isn't it wonderful?"

"I don't know."

"Didn't you ever have a Japanese girl?"

"Yes, but she had to pretend to be Chinese because of the war."

"Well, is it true?"

"She was born in California, it was just the once, I didn't ask her."

"I didn't mean for you to *ask* her. Look at you," she laughed suddenly. "Does *this* make a fool of you, too?" She pushed higher and laughed. "If you want it so badly, if you've got to have it again, if you've got to have more, have all you want."

"You don't have to put ideas in my head."

"I'm not looking at your *head*. Your head's for art and I don't want any part of it. If you've always got to have more, there's always more to have, so why don't you take all you want?"

"I want to read."

"You don't look as if you want to read." She laughed, moved the large round white slowly around, watching his eyes, and him.

He got up, smiling with the surprise he had for her. She still didn't know him. He watched her turn it slowly, her eyes watching him and waiting. She wanted to be quiet now, to let his thinking let her know how to be, and then she felt the sharp sting of his open hand. She screamed, felt it again, screamed again, laughing, leaped to her feet, and ran away. He caught her, and she felt it again, only harder. Again, laughing and calling him dog, and again, until she began to plead with him to stop, and then began to cry, hurt and wanting to hide, crying to herself. He lighted a cigarette and asked if she had been terribly surprised.

"You dog. You dirty crook, I thought you were going to be nice. You hurt me, you really hurt me, I'll never get pregnant again from the way you hurt me, you hurt me everywhere, where I get pregnant even, you dirty dog, you'll never have any more children from me, I thought you wanted to play, I thought you were going to be nice, I didn't care about the first one or the second one but the others hurt me, you dirty dog."

"Take it easy. You'll wake up the kids."

"Don't talk to me any more."

She was mad now, not crying any more, just mad because he'd broken up the play that promised to be so wonderful. Mad because he had done such a thing when she had been having so much fun watching how it was making a fool of him again, done it on purpose, to make a fool of her.

"And don't come near me."

The play was gone out of her voice. She was going now and going fast, because he'd broken it up.

"Don't ever come near me again. I can be like other wives, too, you know."

"Shut up."

"And don't you dare say shut up to me again."

"Shut up."

The woman began to cry again, only this time it was the big beautiful baby bawling, bawling the way she had bawled when he had told her so long ago in New York to go home and not bother herself about him any more, told her he had work to do, told her to go back to the boys who didn't have work to do, and she went, but an hour later when he stepped out of his apartment to take a walk and pick up the morning papers, there she was sitting on the marble bench just outside his door bawling and blubbering, her eyes red, her face red, her mouth wet with slobber, and he thought, Have I got this whole thing wrong? Is it possible that this girl is so much more than she seems to be? Am I so stupid as not to have found out anything about her at all after all this time?

"I was going to go in a minute," she wept. "I was just going to go."

"What are you crying about?"

"I don't know. I don't know, but I wish you knew how it is."

Is it possible? he thought. I've treated her the way I believed she deserved to be treated, like a vagrant piece. What the devil is this?

"Well, come back in here and wash your face. Then I'll walk you home if that's where you want to go."

"I don't want to go home," she wept. "I never want to go home again. I want to stay here the rest of my life."

"This apartment's twenty-five dollars a day. I'm leaving it in a few days to go into the Army."

"I want to go with you," she wept, only she wasn't trying to be funny, she was just sick, he couldn't imagine how she could ever have gotten so sick. He could imagine her getting sick of him as he had gotten sick of her—until now—until this incredible unbelievable bawling that was impossible to disbelieve, for nothing seemed to stop it, not even cold water splashed on her face. What the devil was she bawling *about?*

And why had she picked him to hear it? All he had wanted was another piece, a better one than most for being younger and prettier and funnier, so what was all the bawling about?

Now, in San Francisco, seven years later, she was bawling that way again because in the midst of play he had tricked her, driven the play far back into her and brought forward the weeping to take its place.

"Now, stop that bawling," he said.

But the woman couldn't stop it, it was the one thing over which she had no control, the one thing that made him helpless, the one thing that held them together, pathetically. He got in bed beside her and took her in his arms.

"You dirty dog," she wept, hugging him quickly and kicking her feet around him, to hold him with *them,* too. "I'm so God-damn lonely, and so are you. And down the hall are the two kids we've got, and we're all so God-damn lonely. God, how we must stink."

"Why don't you try to shut up once in a while?"

CHAPTER
9

It was the little boy standing over him, he knew. He had been standing there a minute or two. He always knew in his sleep when the boy arrived, but the boy never did anything and he never said anything. He just stood there, and then his father opened his eyes and got up. His father opened them now.

"Don't you want to go back to bed and sleep some more?"

"No, Papa. I want to get dressed."

"Is Rosey asleep?"

"Asleep? She woke *me* up."

He found his watch on the night table between the two beds and saw that it was a little before seven, not so bad at that. He got out of bed and saw the boy's whole face wink, all the dark of it fall away under the light of gladness.

"O.K., come on."

The boy stopped to look at his mother. Her freckles were out, the way they always were in the morning, her hair was tangled all over, red over the white of her face and neck and shoulders, and her mouth was a little open, a little wet with the drooling she always did when she was asleep.

"Do you want to get in bed with Mama?"

"No, I want to get dressed."

36

"Does Rosey want to get in bed with Mama?"

"She's trying to get dressed. She's got my pants on like a coat."

The boy was angry at his sister but at the same time amused. They had had trouble, the same trouble they had every morning when the girl woke up and plagued the boy to notice her, to let her get in his bed, to go with her up the hall and into the living room as they were forbidden to do, to get going.

The boy knew the man would know that he had hit the girl again and perhaps tell him not to do that, but the man was looking at Mama, he was looking at his wife, and he was smiling a little.

The man and the boy were naked, exactly alike, but the man was huge and hairy and all his skin was pale, and the boy was little, like a little rock, his skin dark and smooth with the darkness and smoothness of a new thing, of the man started out all over again in his son. They were each up a little where they were men, and the man said, "When you get up in the morning go and pee."

"I *did*."

"Did you lift the seat?"

"I always lift the seat."

"Somebody's been peeing on the seat."

"It's Rosey, and it's not pee, it's water. She fills the glass and pours it into the toilet bowl and she never lifts the seat. She says she's peeing like me."

"O.K., let's go."

They found the little girl sitting on the floor between her crib and the boy's bed. She was naked except for the boy's pants which she was trying to get over her head. She had been thoughtful, as she was when she was asleep, until she had seen him with her brother and then she had laughed and got up and run to him.

"Hello, Papa."

He took her up and carried her to the bathroom, where he went over her with a washcloth made warm but without soap. He rinsed the cloth and warmed it and wrung it out again and handed it to the boy, who finished using it in five seconds. The man then used it himself and took them back to their bedroom.

"All right. Stand right there, Rosey. Don't move."

"All right, Papa."

"You, too, Johnny. That's right. Straight. You both look fine. Now don't move. I'm going to put my clothes on and I'll be right back. Don't move, just stand straight that way and wait."

He was dressed in not much more than forty-five seconds. When he got back to the room the girl was sitting on the floor working with the pants again and the boy was looking for something under his bed. They both jumped up and stood somewhat as they had been standing when he had left.

"O.K. Rosey first. Where's your stuff, Rosey?"

"This is all I got," the little girl said, holding out her brother's pants.

He found her stuff all around the room and in her crib but had trouble finding one sock and then found it in the pocket of the pants.

"How did that get in there?"

"Johnny put it in."

"I didn't. She did."

"And he hit me."

"Did you?"

"It wasn't my fault."

The girl was dressed now.

"All right, Rosey. You go over there and look out the window until I get Johnny dressed."

"He hit me, Papa."

"Did it hurt?"

"Yes, Papa," the girl said softly.

"I didn't hit her hard," the boy said. "I just hit her a little one to stop her from putting her sock in my pocket."

"It hurt, Papa."

"Do you want me to spank him?"

"Spank him and spank him and spank him."

He waited a moment, then she said, as she always did, "But not *really*, Papa."

Christ, the man thought, they're crazy about each other.

The boy bent over the man's knee and the man began to let him have it, easy but not too easy because it was no fun for them at all if there wasn't a little noise. They both laughed, laughing together while the man thought, If only this girl would never cry as her mother cries, if only she'd never *need* to, if only it could be so.

The girl threw herself on the man and held the arm he was spanking the boy with.

"Don't spank him, Papa," she said. She wasn't finished yet with the laughter of the game but she was never more in earnest. "Don't spank him. He's my brother," she said.

She hugged the boy, who looked down at her indifferently, his whole face winking, and the girl said, "My little brother. My little baby. Don't cry."

The boy turned and looked at his father. His lips moved a little because it was killing him, he liked it, he wasn't above it, but she was so little and such a crook, provoking him into hitting her all the time, and then when he got in trouble about it, real trouble, not like this game, she came to him when it was all over and said, "I'm sorry, Johnny." And hugged him and told him not to cry, the way she was telling him now when he *wasn't* crying.

The man dressed the boy quickly and turned them loose in the back yard to fool around with the junk out there until he had breakfast ready. The fierce passion of the two of them together began the minute they were alone, the loving and bothering of one another, of dominating one another, each trying new methods or using tried and tested ones. But in the end the boy hit the girl, the girl burst into tears, and the boy stood around feeling sick with guilt because of the awful noise she always made.

He got the oranges out of the bowl above the kitchen sink and went to work getting their juice. Then he got the cold cereal into the bowls and poured sugar and milk into each bowl, called them, and they came climbing up the steps.

He began to get his coffee going in the percolator while they drank their orange juice and fooled around with the cold cereal, not eating it but playing games with it. Then he got the fat bacon going because he knew they never could resist that, at least, and he put a couple of eggs into some water to boil because sometimes they would go to work and actually eat a whole egg, or maybe even two of them, as if they were really hungry, but mainly they were poor eaters, and he and his wife had made a mess of their eating, his wife using the one-for-Papa, one-for-Mama, one-for-Jesus technique, and the man telling them how the kids in Europe didn't have hardly anything to eat, ever. But the boy always said, "Give them my food, Papa."

Well, he wasn't going to fight them about their eating any more. He himself, when he thought of it, as he always did when the boy wouldn't eat, had never been able to get enough, but he had always tried to be polite and had often refused a second helping of something he wanted badly, but this was only when there were strangers around. The rest of the time he ate all he could get, and it wasn't that way with his son. It wasn't that way with his daughter, either. Kids just don't like to eat very much these days, he thought. It was true of everybody's kids. Everybody was having trouble with their kids about eating.

Maybe the kids know what they're doing, he thought.

Right now, though, his own kids were playing games of leverage, and pouring with their spoons the milk and the cereal that was mushy now, but to hell with it, he thought, maybe the games mean more to them than eating the lousy food. Maybe if somebody fixed them a bowl of hot oatmeal or something, they'd eat, but that was nonsense, too, because he had tried it and they had both insisted on cold cereal. Why? Because they could have more fun pouring the cold cereal, that's why. He saw the girl lift her bowl and pour half of it onto the linoleum, but he decided to let that go, too. She liked to do that.

"O.K.," he said. "Bacon. This for you, Rosey. This for you, Johnny. And that's all."

"There's more," Johnny said.

"That's for me."

He saw them quickly eat the crisp bacon he had given them, and then the boy said, "I want some more."

"That's for Papa," the girl said.

"He can make some more. This isn't Europe."

He gave the boy some more.

"You want some more, Rosey?"

"No, Papa. It's yours. Johnny's a bad boy."

"O.K. You can have an egg."

He broke open an egg and worked the stuff out with a teaspoon into a dish with a little butter in it and set the dish in front of the girl, lifting away her bowl of cereal and eating what was in it, and then eating what was left in the boy's bowl, too.

"You're a garbage can," the boy said. He'd gotten that from his mother and he knew the man didn't mind hearing it whenever he gobbled up their leftovers.

"It's good food. Why waste it?"

He got an egg to the boy, too, and sure enough the going was a little better than it had been for several days. They ate all the bacon and all the egg, but hell, there was no use pretending, they weren't eaters, they just fooled around at it a little three times a day. They didn't run to it. They looked at it out of the corners of their eyes and never seemed to think much of it.

The day was a pretty good one, too. It was foggy of course, as it almost always is in San Francisco, especially out where they were, so near the ocean, but the sun was sending light and heat through the mist, and they could have themselves a time in the yard.

They went down again and he fetched the morning paper from just inside the metal gate on the sidewalk that locked in the exposed stairway, and then he poured himself a cup of coffee and began to look at the day's news.

The boy was the first to come up.

"Number two," he said.

The man didn't say anything and the boy went along, singing *Just a love mess,* which was his version of *love nest.*

The girl was up before the boy had finished.

"Is it Rosey?" the boy called out from the bathroom.

"Yes, Johnny," the girl said.

"What do you want?"

"Number one or number two?" the man said to the girl.

"Three."

"O.K .Wait till Johnny gets out of there."

Of course the girl didn't wait, because all she wanted was to be in there, too, to be near him, to make him angry by getting the glass and filling it with water.

They were back in the yard again after ten minutes of quiet fighting in the bathroom, and then it was the girl again.

"When is Mama getting up?"

"Pretty soon. Go downstairs and play."

"All right, Papa," but she didn't go, she sat down in her small chair at the small table and put part of the morning paper that had fallen to the floor on the table in front of her and looked at it.

Around ten his wife ran naked to the bathroom. On her way back, when she saw him in the living room standing beside the small piano looking at a book, she waited until he looked up from the book. Then, she lifted her arms, half stretching and half teasing.

"Get dressed, will you? I've got to go upstairs and get to work."

"O.K. I'll only be a minute. You were sweet last night. I mean, the second time when I felt so bad. Do you love me?"

"If I don't, we'd better try to find out what it is that's knocking the hell out of me. I can't write any more. I don't even like the *idea* of writing. I can't read, either. I think all writing stinks."

The woman went to the man and wrapped her arms around him, but the man went right on reading.

"You know what?" she whispered in his ear. "The first one was the best, though. It was the best ever."

"Sure it was. Now, will you get dressed? I've got to get going."

The woman clutched him to confirm what didn't need to be confirmed, laughed, and ran to get dressed. The man went from the lower flat where they lived to the upper flat where he worked, and where he and the woman lived when there was a nanny for the kids.

CHAPTER
10

The upper flat was a shambles, but it always was. It smelled of stale cigarette smoke because he smoked so much whenever he worked or tried to. It smelled of not being lived in, too, and of fog and books. Books he hadn't had a chance to look into yet, some of them on hand for months, not even unwrapped yet, piled on the floor and on the furniture. There were stacks of magazines mixed in with the books, mail, and manuscripts, pebbles and twigs and roots and branches of trees washed smooth and clean by the sea that he kept bringing home all the time. The pebbles were in small piles on the floor and furniture of every room in that flat, or in water in glass bowls because their color came out in water, and the twigs and roots and branches were leaning wherever he had found a place for them when he had first brought them home. There were rocks, too, chalk-white ones, brown, black, green and blue, most of them more or less egg-shaped but a few of them flat or round, and these were strewn about all over, too, excepting those that were serving as paperweights.

He lifted the porous brown one that he was so fond of, that he had found at low tide in a cove somewhere south of Big Sur on Highway One, a cove he had driven back over

Highway One a year later expressly to find again because he had wanted to see if he could find out what was so wonderful about it, to make him remember it so much, to think about it so much, but he hadn't found it, the sea had come up and hidden it and he had driven on, saying to the woman, "I can't tell you how bad it makes me feel that I can't find that cove."

The cove was hundreds of millions of pebbles just a little smaller than jelly beans all gathered together on a downward-slanting beach just beneath red clay cliffs three and four feet high with larger pebbles in smaller groups here and there, and now and then extraordinarily handsome rocks, all of them bright in the light, all of them a little wet yet, with seaweed strewn about over and among them, and little forms of life dead or dying or hurrying off to live some more among them, jelly things, leaf things, grass things, shell things, but nothing anywhere of man's, no tin cans, no bottles, no broken glass, no paper, just the cove loaded with treasures which nearly maddened him to see, the air smelling of clay, wet rock, water and sea life.

It was ten or eleven in the morning, or at any rate sometime before noon, and he had been driving through thick fog since two in the morning, they hadn't gone to bed at all that night although they had planned to, they'd had a nanny then, and they had planned to go to bed at midnight and get up at five for an early start, but the woman had said, "Let's start now, let's not sleep at all, let's just get in the car and go." He was on his way that instant, going down the stairs from the top flat with the suitcases. They had had breakfast at the only place open in Monterey, ham and eggs and a lot of coffee, but it had only made them sleepy, so that after Big Sur the woman had asked him to please stop soon so she could go to sleep in the car.

"O.K.," he said, "just let me find a place to get the car off the highway."

An hour or so later he found the cove. He was there more than an hour while his wife slept, and then she got up and took off her shoes and stockings and went to him where he was gathering pebbles and rocks.

"The back of the car is full of them," he said.

"What do you want them for?"

"You know I keep pebbles and rocks to look at," he said. "Look at this one."

He handed her the brown one he was now holding.

The woman held the rock and said, "Do you love me?"

"I *stopped* so you could sleep, didn't I? Of course I love you. But don't you love anything else?"

"*Than* what?"

"Than me or you or whatever it is that you keep asking about all the time?"

"I love you and that's all."

"If you love somebody, you love other things, too, don't you? You love everything, don't you?"

"Not me. Just you, just me, just Johnny, just Rosey, but mainly you, or mainly me, or you *and* me. Isn't that what it comes to?"

"Yes, I guess it is, at that. Even so, I never saw a place like this before. A man could look for a place like this his whole life and never find it."

"It *is* nice, but I'm hungry."

"We'll eat at the next town. But don't rush me. I want to stay here awhile. I like it here. I don't suppose I could buy this cove."

"Would you like to buy the ocean, too?"

"Yes, I would."

"And the sun. Would you like to buy that, too?"

"Yes, the sun, too."

"Well, when you get to Hollywood, just go out and meet the clever agents who are always talking so big and sit down with them and let them be clever for you, so you can get a lot of money and buy anything you want."

"If money could do anything like that for anybody, I'd go after it harder."

"Are you trying to tell me to be satisfied with the ocean

46

and the sun? I'll bet that's what you're trying to do, and I thought I was kidding *you*."

"I'm not kidding. I'd like to buy this cove, that's all."

"It doesn't belong to anybody anyway. You can have as much of it as you like any time you like."

"It's the nicest place I've ever been. I wish I could stay here."

"Well, you can't."

"I know."

"I'll gather some, too."

She gathered a couple of dozen small ones, but they weren't very good because she hadn't had any experience with pebbles and didn't know what to look for. The ones that were immortal were the ones to look for, the ones color and shape *said* were immortal. The ones that were art, that were sculpture, that were whole.

She was a good girl, though, she just didn't know about pebbles. She wanted him to like the ones she'd gathered, so he did, he told her they were great, she hadn't gone back to the car and turned on the radio, she had put up with it, she had tried, she was great sometimes, sometimes she could be something made out of light and time and water, like one of the pebbles, sometimes she could shut up and go along, tag along with him even when her common sense told her he was going nowhere, sometimes she thought about things and decided there might be something to them at that, nothing much but something, a little something, and she looked fine, she looked younger than her few years, sleepy and grave and troubled and thoughtful, the way the little girl always looked when she went to sleep.

"Are they really good ones?"

"They are."

"What makes the good ones?"

"Picking them up. Noticing them and picking them up and keeping them, that's what does it."

Now, in the upper flat he put the big porous brown rock aside and took up the papers that were the work he was doing. It was desperate work and it stank. He put the work back on the table and went to the window to look down at the street. The street stank, too. He just didn't know where to start. What he wanted was money. What they needed was money. What they didn't have was money. What they had was the kids and debts.

He dialed the number of the telephone downstairs and when the woman got on he said, "I'll tell you what. I've just figured out how we can get hold of all the money we need. We can sell the kids."

"Do you love me?" the woman said.

"I telephoned you, didn't I? I left my work to telephone you. Take good care of the kids. Give them a good lunch and clean up the joint a little. The whole house is a shambles."

"What are *you* going to do?"

"I'll come down and help you after a while. We'll have some coffee when they're having their naps. Phone me when they're asleep."

CHAPTER
11

He saw the mail-carrier coming down the street, so he went down to the street-level basement where the mail was dropped. The shelves along the entire far wall were loaded with books and magazines, the baby grand pianola was there beside the gas furnace, the pianola that had been in his last play on Broadway, the flop, the third in a row. The car was there, and all the junk from New York: the baby carriages and other things with wheels that small children were pushed around in, the cribs and canvas bathing tubs for infants, the toys, the tricycles, and the boy's bicycle that he couldn't ride yet from the seat but could somehow ride, that he loved so much but could only have when someone was there to help and see that he didn't hurt himself. The garden tools, the pruning shears for the rose trees and bushes, the shovel and rake, the lawnmower.

Christ, he thought, I ought to get up at seven and be at work in an office in town somewhere by nine and come home at six, and live the way everybody else around here does.

One day when he was cutting the lawn and letting Johnny help—it was sundown then, about seven in the evening—a man came out of the top flat of a house just like his house across the way and called out to him, "What are you writing?"

The mail was good-for-nothing.

A woman in Richmond, Virginia, wrote to say that he had twice described someone as being cultured when the correct term was cultivated. The woman asked if he had done this on purpose, as part of his style, or because he didn't know any better.

The lecture-bureau man who had been writing him for five years wrote again saying that he could arrange for a very profitable series of lectures at a moment's notice, in almost any part of the country, including the Far West.

There was a royalty statement from his publisher which only reminded him that he was still in debt, even though the books had sold fairly well over a period of six months.

There was an invitation from a cousin who lived four or five miles across town to go to the races at Bay Meadows and make a killing.

There was a check for twenty-seven dollars and eighty-one cents, which represented his share of royalties from an anthology of one-act plays.

There was a letter from a girl who had been eleven years old when she had appeared in one of his plays but was now eighteen, and there was a snapshot of her in the letter. She wore a low-cut evening dress so that he could see how nicely she had grown and she said she never would forget him for picking her out of all the others and giving her her start in the theater. She was in Hollywood now, and when was he going to go there and show them how to make moving pictures? She said her mother sent him her love and hoped he would visit them in their nice apartment when he got to Hollywood.

And there was a letter for his wife from her friend Lucretia in New York.

He put the letter with the small check in it and the one with the snapshot in it in the back pocket of his trousers, and then went up to the lower flat and let himself in with a key, calling out to the woman first so that she wouldn't be frightened. He handed her the mail, because she liked to look at everything.

"Is this all?"

"What's Lucretia say?"

"Are you sure you haven't kept out some of the mail?"

"Go ahead. Open it and see what she's up to."

The woman tore open the fine envelope with the fancy writing all over it and glanced quickly at the first of the five or six pages of very thin paper, and then she said, "They're coming out to pay us a visit."

"The hell they are."

"They can stay upstairs."

"They can shit. That's where I work. Now, listen, I don't want any trouble about your friends. Things are tough enough without a couple of phonies coming out here."

"They have to go to Hollywood. They only want to stop and say hello."

"Hello for a week? Write and tell her I'm working. I've got to get to work and you know I'll never be able to with them around. It takes time to get ready to work and you're always arranging for something to happen that will stop me from ever getting ready."

"Can't they come for just a *little* visit? She's my best friend and he's such a great man."

"She's a bore and he's a bore."

"I never see anybody out here. Just the people you know. None of my people."

"Your people stink. Your sister was here for ten days a month ago. Two months before that your mother was here. Now don't try to make me put up with these two, too."

"O.K. I'll write and tell her the kids are sick, but I think you're mean."

"The kids aren't sick. Tell her I'm working. She'll understand."

"I can't be rude."

"It's not rude to tell the truth. I *am* working. We're broke. I've got to see about getting hold of some money."

51

"O.K., I'll tell her you're working."

"Now, don't fool around the way you did about your sister. Don't have her drop in on us and then give me a long explanation about how you must have misdirected the letter telling her not to come because she hadn't received it, and now as long as she was here, we couldn't turn her away. Don't do anything like that again. That was a dirty trick."

"She didn't get the letter."

"If she didn't, you didn't write a letter."

"You saw me mail the letter yourself."

"Then you didn't tell her not to come. You told her something else. Maybe you told her to pretend that she hadn't gotten the letter. All I know is that we agreed that you would write and tell her not to come because I was working, and then a taxi came up to the house and there she was with six suitcases all the way from New York. No more of that."

"O.K."

"Just take care of your kids and let me see if I can start writing again."

"I miss my people."

"Your kids are your people now."

He went out and up the stairs and back to his worktable, but it was no use, he had no heart for the work, he had been fighting the idea of abandoning it for days, and now he knew it was abandoned. He'd worked eight days for nothing. It was the tenth or eleventh job he had abandoned in ten or eleven weeks. Well, he would have to start again and this time see that it was not a false start. But when he tried to think what would not be a false start, he could think of nothing that wouldn't, everything would be a false start, anything anybody might do would be a false start, there was no such thing as a true start.

He took the envelope with the snapshot in it, put a match to it, and tossed it into the fireplace. Then he got the check out of the other envelope and put it in his wallet to have when he went to the bank.

CHAPTER
12

The way things were, he wished his profession wasn't writing, but that was silly, writing *was* his profession, it had always been his profession, only now he didn't want to write, didn't want to try to write, never reached his worktable eager to see what he had written the previous day, the way it had been in the old days, all he wanted was money because he always needed money, maybe if he had enough of it once and for all, enough to pay his debts, and buy a house somewhere where she could feel more at home, in Manhattan maybe, or Long Island, or Connecticut, maybe then she would feel at home and be able to get along with a nanny and herself and the kids and himself.

Maybe then he'd be able to get along with her, help her over the hard times a little better, find out why she had to bite her fingernails and be in despair so often, maybe if he could get hold of enough money all of a sudden, *that* would be how he would be able to forget all about money and be free to think about her only, and the kids, and the work, and never again need to be harassed.

Maybe then she wouldn't be forever discontented, wanting a better house, better clothes, better times, and all the other things she seemed to be dreaming about all the time, maybe then she wouldn't feel she was losing her youth and beauty for nothing, she'd calm down and see that what she had was just about as much as any woman could ever get, and maybe she'd be thankful for it and make the most of it and not go off by herself in her head dreaming up desperate ways to make up for the loss of her youth and beauty, writing to her friends as if she were writing from a penitentiary, asking them to visit her, for God's sake come and see her, telegraphing them, screaming at them at the top of her voice on the telephone, and then, after talking about hats and shoes and dresses and who'd laid who and why, hanging up on a bill for thirty-six dollars and seventy-five cents, wandering around in despair, unable to fix a simple supper for the kids, or make a sandwich for herself, or think of anything to do.

Maybe if he could get hold of thirty thousand dollars straight off and be out of debt and have enough left over for a new house for her and five hundred dollars to go in her pocket for anything she felt like buying, everything might straighten out and he might be able to get ready to work, and then actually write again.

He couldn't get to work the way things were because he couldn't get *ready* to. He was willing to believe that it was just as important to work for the family, for the kids and for her, as it was to work at his profession, but the way things were he just couldn't afford not to try to work at his profession, too. If he was rich, he'd be glad to help her all the time and let his work go.

There's the typewriter, he thought. Sit down and write.

He put paper into the machine and began to work, but after an hour he knew it wouldn't do. He wasn't ready. He couldn't work until he was ready. The only way he could get ready was for her to feel at home and to know something about her kids and about him and about love and about fun, and she either just couldn't feel at home or wouldn't, she wouldn't stop biting her fingernails and going off into despair, making any work he was trying to do seem hopeless and useless, she could only have the fun they were always having and then go right back into homelessness.

Writing had always been a fight, but for a long time he had always believed he could win the fight. He had plunged in and tried, but sooner or later the fight had always been too much for him. He had always believed he could write under any circumstance, any set of circumstances, but he had found that he couldn't.

He could still read a little, but he was finding a lot of fault with everything he was reading, too.

He was trying to think of an entire work, something that would turn out to be full, that he could do in two or three months, when she let herself in and said, "What you doing?"

"I'm trying to think of something to write in two or three months in short daily installments."

"I wish you knew how much he admires you."

"Who?"

"Leander."

"They can't come, and I don't want to hear any more about it."

"He told me you're the greatest writer in America."

"For your own sake, stop lying, will you?"

"It's not a lie. He told me at a party, when you were overseas."

"Well, I don't want them here, that's all. If they come to town, you can take a taxi and spend an afternoon and evening with them."

"Can I? You *said* I could. Don't take it back."

"O.K."

"And you'll let me buy a new dress so I won't look like a dog when I see them? Nothing expensive, just something new, something under fifty dollars."

"O.K."

"And you'll come downstairs and stay with the kids so I can go to the beauty parlor?"

"O.K."

"I mean, now. My appointment's for eleven and it's already ten after."

"When did you make it?"

"Half an your ago."

"Why? You've got to get the kids their lunch and get them to bed for their naps."

"Oh, won't you do it for me, just this once?"

"Why not make the appointment for tomorrow when they're napping, the way you always do once a week when you go to the beauty parlor?"

"Well, after I'm finished at the beauty parlor I thought I'd buy the dress. I don't have to have cash for it. I'll charge it."

"O.K., let's have it. What are you trying to tell me?"

"They'll be here tomorrow morning. I telephoned and told them to go to the Fairmont because—"

"The kids are sick?"

"I just couldn't tell them you were working. They'd never understand. And Rosey *has* a running nose."

"O.K."

They went downstairs to the lower flat.

"Could you let me have some money for the taxi and beauty parlor?"

"O.K."

He gave her two tens and a five, but she wanted more, so he gave her another ten. The doorbell rang and when he opened it he saw that it was a taxi-driver. The woman kissed him and said, "About five, I guess, but maybe a little later."

"O.K."

He went to the kitchen and looked into the refrigerator to see what might be possible for their lunch, and then into the cupboard, the vegetable bin, and everywhere that food was kept. There wasn't much, but there was enough. He'd give them breakfast again, or some soup out of a can, and mashed potatoes. The back door was open but he couldn't hear them fighting, so he went out onto the steps and saw that they were lying under an army blanket talking quietly and looking up, either at the sky or at the top of their house or at the houses all around or at nothing. The neighbor on the left, Turandi Turanda, was working quietly in his vegetable garden. Either they had already had their fun with him or they hadn't noticed that he had stepped out of his house, for they always talked with him, the boy climbing the fence and hanging on to see over it, the girl getting up on an apple box to look over and watch and talk, too.

He stepped back into the kitchen and began to peel the potatoes. By the time they were boiling he heard the three of them talking. The man was more or less retired, a plasterer by trade, so he spent a lot of time in his garden, and he either liked the kids or put up with them because they were always there and there was nothing he could do about it. Sometimes he lifted the little girl and walked around with her in his garden and the boy hoisted himself over the fence and let himself down, falling part of the way, and skinning his hands a little. They seemed to be friends, the three of them, and the man's wife (whenever she came out into the yard) talked with them and admired the girl and teased the boy about putting him in a hole in the ground. But it was all play, and the boy only hollered at her because he knew she would never put him in a hole in the ground.

Their voices grew louder, so he stepped to the door to see what it was about. Turandi Turanda was standing at the fence, looking down at them and talking. The boy was holding a tennis ball and the girl wanted it but he wouldn't let her have it.

"You be a good boy, Johnny," Turanda said. "You give her the ball. You got other things."

The boy handed the ball to the girl.

"Shit," he said.

Turanda looked around to see if anybody had heard, and then he said, "There, Rosey, see? Johnny's a good boy. Tell him thanks."

"Shit," the girl said. She said it softly and sweetly, like a beautiful word. "Thanks, Johnny, my little brother."

The neighbor went back to his garden, and the man thought, I've got to lay off letting them hear words like that.

But it was hard not to keep saying words like that all the time.

He got them their lunch and told them Mama had gone shopping for supper and he took off their clothes and put them in their beds and then sat down in the living room and went on thinking about money. He turned on the radio to the station that gave the race results and listened to the music that came in between, and then to the results at two Eastern tracks. He got the morning paper and turned to the sports page and studied the entries at all the tracks and figured that if he bet two hundred dollars across the board and just happened to get a winner he would be able to drive to town sometime that afternoon and pick up anywhere from a thousand to two or three thousand, and maybe with that make a beginning.

He picked a horse in the next race at both of the Eastern tracks and when the announcer gave the results, one of the horses won and paid sixteen forty, eight twenty and five forty, and the other one ran third and paid four forty.

He did some more brooding and then picked a horse named Sugar, at four to one in the fifth at Arlington. He telephoned the bookie where his credit was good and bet the horse two hundred across the board. He sat and waited for the radio man to give the results, smoking one cigarette after another and feeling sick because all he had in the bank was a hundred and forty dollars.

The horse wasn't in the money, so he bet a horse in the seventh, but that horse ran third, so he owed the bookie eight hundred and twenty instead of twelve hundred, which is what he would have owed if the horse had run out of the money. But that wasn't winning, that wasn't even getting out of debt to the bookie, let alone out of debt to all of the people he had borrowed money from, so he bet a horse in the last race at one of the Eastern tracks but that horse wasn't in the money either, so now he owed the bookie fourteen hundred and twenty.

He bet three hundred across the board on a horse named

Me First in the first race at Bay Meadows, post position one, Longden up, maiden three-year-olds, six furlongs, so if Me First didn't get in the money he would owe the bookie twenty-three hundred and twenty, which meant that he would have to borrow twenty-five hundred from somebody, only there wasn't anybody to borrow from.

But the horse won and paid a pretty good price. The man got up and walked around, even though he hadn't figured his winnings yet. When he figured them he was astonished to discover that they came to so much: eighteen hundred and eighty dollars, net. Well, he couldn't pay his debts with it, but at least he *had* it, and it was better than needing to go out and try to borrow twenty-five hundred. He got into the shower, then put on fresh clothes, and felt a little easier.

He had been in another tough spot and again he had gotten out of it. Now, instead of having only a hundred and forty dollars, he had a little better than two thousand. He could bet another horse and maybe win again, but to hell with it. All he wanted was to get something, and he had, he'd gotten more than he had expected to get, so it was enough. Maybe if he could have a little luck every day like that he could get hold of enough money to pay the debts and have something left over for the other things.

He dressed the kids and put the girl in her chair in the car and drove to town. He put the car in the garage a block and a half from the bookie's and asked the man to fill the tank and check the oil and water. He told the kids he was going to get a package of cigarettes and would be back in a minute, and not to move. He went up to the bookie's and chatted with the boys a few minutes and then Leo looked into his book and said, "Eighteen eighty, right?" and counted the money out and thanked him.

He took the money and put it in his pocket and chatted with the boys some more, and then he got up and went back to the car.

The kids were laughing together about something.

He paid the man and drove out Geary to the ocean, along

the ocean four or five miles, and then he stopped where some new houses were being built and he and the boy piled scraps of lumber in the back of the car for the fireplace because doing that made the boy happier than anything else he knew how to do. He drove home and left the car out front and took the kids for a walk to a drugstore and got them each and himself an ice-cream soda.

It wouldn't be so bad if he could get hold of money that way any time he needed it.

CHAPTER
13

He was clean and calm sitting with the kids in the booth in the ice-cream-parlor part of the drugstore and that's what a man wanted, that's what he always wanted, to be clean and calm, his kids across a table from him with their new eyes, new voices, hands and fingers, hair and lips, teeth and nostrils and ears, moisture and skin, their new beating hearts and working lungs, that's all any man ever wanted, just to be decently at peace with himself and his woman and to have his kids around and happy about vanilla and chocolate and soda, the long spoon and the straws, and the drama of other people around, the druggist, the girl who brought the stuff, the boy who made it, and the other people having other stuff.

All any man ever wanted was peace and the only way he could have it was to have money, and now he had a little. Betting the races was the best way to get money if you had to get it that way at all. You never hurt anybody by winning on the races because whatever you got you got anonymously and whoever lost because he had picked another horse in the same race was unknown to you. It was a dirty business, but if you won, it certainly made a lot of difference.

He asked the kids if they would like to go to the notion

store across the street and have a look at the junk, and they said they did, so they went there and he let them have one thing each because having too much, or being free to have too much, made them unhappy, confused them, so the girl had a blown-up balloon that was red on a stick, and the boy had a gyroscope in a square pasteboard box. They stepped out into the street and began to move homeward, but the man noticed that the old North Carolina barber whose shop had only one chair had nobody in it, so he asked the kids if they would sit nicely while he got a haircut and they said they would, so he got a haircut. Then he stepped into the Safeway, to the butcher's, and bought four thick sirloins and six French lamb chops but didn't buy anything else because you had to stand in line to pay and have your stuff wrapped everywhere except at the butcher's. In the delicatessen next door that the lady who loved her big ugly cat and was always making rugs out of rags and listening to the radio owned he bought six cans of chili with beans, and that was enough to carry, so they walked home. He and the boy unloaded the pieces of lumber from the car to the basement. He took up an armful, put them in the fireplace and lighted the fire because they all liked to see a fire.

The red balloon popped and the little girl looked astonished, as she always did when a balloon popped.

"It was my balloon," she said. "I want my balloon."

She held what was left of it, the thin limp absurd-looking rubber and the skinny stick, and she didn't like it. The man examined the wreckage, got a piece of string and tied some of the rubber together. He undid the neck from the stick to which it was attached and blew into it and the little girl saw the balloon again, but different, tied, lopsided, the color different, ends hanging loose, but she laughed and liked it. The man tied the neck, and the girl waited to have her balloon again. When she had it she squeezed it and let it fall and bounce, but the boy just sat and watched the fire.

"What is fire?" he said.

"What we see there."

"But what is it?"

"What it *really* is I don't know," the man said. "But I know that the sun in the sky is fire."

"It's my balloon," the girl said. "Johnny can't have it."

"I got this," the boy said. He lifted the square pasteboard box containing the gyroscope. "Whatever it is."

"It's a gyroscope."

"What does it do?"

"It turns."

"What's it *for?*"

"To look at when it turns. It's beautiful then."

The boy lifted the top off the square pasteboard box and turned the box over so that the gyroscope would come out into his hand. He held it up and looked at it.

The girl squeezed the lopsided balloon, rubbed it against her face, tossed it up, watched it fall. The boy looked at the gyroscope and then let it rest on the floor and looked back at the fire. He had been sitting on the floor. Now he stretched out full length on his belly, rested his chin in his right hand. The man poked the fire and put more wood on it, squares and angles of house lumber, all kinds of shapes piled together.

"It looks like a church burning," the boy said.

The man looked to see if this was so, and it was, it *did* look like a church burning.

"But nobody's in it," the boy said. "They never burn churches with people in them. They always get the people out and then burn them, so the people can see the fires. Do they ring the bells when they burn churches?"

"I don't believe they do," the man said. "But when the bells fall they make quite a lot of noise."

"Did you *see* a church burn?"

"Yes, I did. I was a little older than you are now. It was at night and everybody ran. You couldn't go close because it was too hot, but you could see everything because the fire made so much light. You could hear the fire cracking the wood, and things falling inside the church, and then at last

63

the bells fell and rang. We went home then, and the next day it was all black there, like the ashes after a fire burns in a fireplace."

"I don't like it when it's black in the fireplace," the boy said.

They sat and talked quietly for an hour, and then he heard the taxi out front and after a moment the woman let herself in. The taxi-driver carried half a dozen packages. The little girl ran and the woman hugged her and kissed her and talked to her, and then she told the taxi-driver where to put the packages, on her bed. She handed him some currency, and the man tipped his hat and thanked her and went out. The woman closed the door and stood hushed with excitement and happiness.

"Wait till you see the things I've bought."

She picked up the boy and danced around with him and then put him down again.

"Do you like my hair?"

She removed a scarf wrapped over her hair and the red fell down, new and bright.

"It's beautiful, Mama," the boy said.

"Oh, Johnny. Wait till you see Mama's new dress. Shall I put it on now?"

"Yes, Mama."

"Shall I?" the woman said to the man.

"Sure. Let's have a look at it."

The woman hugged the man, ran off to the bedroom, and closed the door, but the little girl opened the door and went in, and then the boy went in, too, and the man heard them talking in there. The woman came out, and she looked fine.

"It cost a hundred, but we've got so many debts anyway I thought you wouldn't care. Do you like it?"

"Yes. You look fine."

"I bought some other things, too. I'll show them to you afterwards."

"O.K."

"They cost about a hundred, too, but they're things I need,

shoes and stockings and brassières and perfume. You won't
make me send them back, will you? It's so humiliating. Just
this once more. I've got everything now."

"No. You can keep them."

"Some women spend a *thousand* for one dress."

"You look fine in this one."

"I thought you'd be angry."

"No, it's O.K. I'm glad you got the stuff."

"Really? How come?"

"Take it off now and get supper for the kids. You and I'll
eat after they're in bed. I've bought lamb chops for them
and sirloins for us."

"All right," the woman said. "Johnny, Rosey, go to your
room and play until Mama gets supper."

The children went down the hall to their room. The
woman closed the door behind them, then came to the man
and put her arms around him and said, "I love you so much.
I love our life together so much. I love Johnny and Rosey
so much."

The man held her gently, then tightly, and kissed her.

"Wait till you see me tonight."

She was happy because she had new things to wear and
she'd been to the beauty parlor and her friends from New
York would be in town tomorrow and she would get all
dressed up and go and see them and let them see her.

CHAPTER
14

The woman made them a good supper of broiled lamb chops, boiled spinach, stewed fruit out of a can, and milk. They didn't finish everything but they did pretty well. She gave them each two teaspoons of the thick brown syrup that was supposed to have everything in it, that they seemed to like to take, that she had been giving them every night after supper for more than a month. It had a name that made it sound like it ought to be something somebody had figured out carefully. The doctor said it was a good thing. He gave it to his own kids, he said. It looked like molasses but didn't smell as good. It didn't smell fishy but it didn't smell like candy, either.

"Can I have a bath tonight?" the boy said.

"Ask Papa."

The boy went into the living room and said, "Can I have a bath tonight, Papa?"

"Ask Mama."

The boy's face winked.

"Papa," he said, "I *asked* Mama. She said ask Papa. I'll ask Rosey."

He ran back to the kitchen, to keep up with the joke.

"Rosey," he said. "Can I have a bath tonight?"

The little girl looked at him sideways, knowing it was a joke.

"Not tonight," she said, "because I'm too tired."

The boy watched her.

"Because you was a bad boy," she said.

He watched some more.

"Because you hit your little sister," she said.

He just had to watch a little longer.

"Because there's no water," she said.

Would there be more?

"Because you're a poopoo," she said.

More?

"Pohpoh," she said.

She ran into the living room with the fun.

"*Isn't* Johnny a pohpoh, Papa?"

"Is he?"

"I *saw* him. He's a pohpoh and a poopoo and a piepie. That's why he can't have a bath tonight. He's a paypay."

"He's a peepee," she said and laughed.

"Peepee?" the boy said. "I'll peepee you if you say *I'm* a peepee."

"Shall I give him a bath?" the woman said. "Shall I give them both a bath? I bathed them both night before last."

"Bathe them," the man said. "I'll straighten out the kitchen."

"What about their sheets? I haven't changed them in days. It must be a week at least."

"Change them. I'll get supper, too."

"All right. If they're going to get clean, they might as well get into clean beds, too. Will you make a green salad, with the wine vinegar from Vanessi's?"

"Sure."

"Yum yum," the woman said, "if you know what I mean."

She's happy all right. She'd be happy all the time if nobody ever had to do anything but have fun and not think about anything else all the time.

She's right, too. She's got a perfect system if it would work. I'd go for that system any day if it would work.

CHAPTER

15

They were eating. It might have been the thousandth time.

"What did you write today?"

"When?"

"This morning, when you went upstairs."

"I've forgotten the precise words, but they were *words*."

"What did you *expect* them to be?"

"That's *all* they were."

"That's all any writing is, isn't it?"

"No, that's precisely what writing *isn't*."

"Well, what were the words *about*, then?"

"Nothing. If writing were words, writing would be easy. Writing is stuff that happens in spite of words. There's no other way for writing to happen than *with* words, but at the same time it's got to happen in spite of them. The thing that gets you in writing is the story the words themselves don't *tell* but make you *know*. It's something like that."

"Well, what did you *think* about, then?"

"I thought about money. It's the only thing I thought about. Most people forget it. I can't. I think about it all the time."

"We need an awful lot, don't we?"

"We need thirty thousand. To *start*, I mean."

"Would that pay the debts and *everything*?"

"Yes. I figured it out on a piece of paper and thirty thousand would pay the debts and leave a little."

"How much?"

"About seven thousand."

"What could we do with *that?*"

"Take it and run. Sit on it. Look at it. Smell it. Put it in silver dollars and stack them up in piles in the living room. I was thinking of paving the hall with them. It wouldn't take more than two thousand and it would make quite an impression on visitors."

"On me, too. What else did you think?"

"I thought if I changed a thousand dollars into dimes—just a measly thousand—this would be petty because they're such small coins."

"What else?"

"I thought if I had a nickel for every dollar I pissed away in my life I'd still be rich because twenty nickels make a dollar and there ought to be about two hundred thousand of them."

"How did you spend two hundred thousand dollars?"

"It was easy."

"You spent most of it before you met me."

"I spent a little after I met you."

"How much?"

"Thirty thousand a year, I suppose."

"Six years. What's that come to?"

"A hundred and eighty thousand."

"Is that all?"

"Maybe it was forty thousand a year. That would make it about two hundred and forty thousand."

"You spent something the year we weren't married, too."

"I would have spent that anyway."

"You would have spent the two hundred and forty thousand anyway, too, wouldn't you have?"

"I don't know. Anyhow maybe it's not the spending that makes the difference, maybe it's whether or not you're earning it to spend, and I'm not. I haven't written anything that has earned anything since I got out of the Army."

"Or since you got in. How many years is that?"

"Three in, three out. Six."

"That's how long we've been married, too. But you haven't written anything that has made any money since we *met*, have you?"

"No, I guess I haven't. The money all came from stuff I wrote before we met."

"I'm hurt. Aren't I inspiring?"

"Awe-inspiring."

"I thought a wife always inspired her husband."

"To think about money."

"Do I spend as much as all *that?*"

"You don't spend much. I just don't write anything. All I do is think about money."

"Do you love money?"

"I *need* money. I don't hate money, but I hate to need it so badly."

"Well, what are we going to do?"

"Be poor, I suppose. Wear out our clothes. Make the most of everything we have. Enjoy the things that don't cost anything or cost only a little. Improve our health. Be happy. Forget money and remember everything else."

"How are we going to pay the debts?"

"Maybe we aren't. At least not for a while. Not until we've forgotten about money for so long that all of a sudden we find that I've written a few things that are worth something."

"Will that happen?"

"It *could* happen, it used to happen all the time."

"I don't like to be poor."

"I know you don't. But it's not nearly as bad as you think."

"I hate being poor."

"It's not so bad. It makes people more alive. Even when I used to get money I never stopped being poor."

"That's silly."

"What happens is that if you let yourself get rich in money, you get poor in living."

"No, you don't. The richer you get in money the richer you get in living and everything else."

"You get poor in living. You get poverty-stricken. The more money you get, the more like a beggar you become. A man who doesn't think about money is a lord. A man who does is a cripple with his hand held out. I think about money all the time. It's humiliating."

"Don't you sometimes think about something else, too?"

"No. Everything else I think about turns out to be money, too."

"Everything?"

"Everything."

"Last night? The first time?"

"The first and second both."

"I think about money a lot, too," the woman said, "but I think more about other things, too."

"It's all money you think about," the man said. "You think you think about other things, too, but you don't. You never do. If you did, you'd be a different person."

"Don't you like the person I am?"

"The person you are isn't an easy person to like."

"Well, you can get a divorce, then."

"No, I can't."

"You can get a divorce any time you feel like it. Get it tomorrow. I don't want to be married to a man who doesn't love me. I don't want a man to make love to me who doesn't love me. Get a divorce tomorrow. Why can't you get a divorce tomorrow?"

"I can't afford it."

"Get a divorce tomorrow."

"I can't leave the kids, either."

"You can leave *me*, but you can't leave the kids. Get your lousy divorce tomorrow."

"I can't, and shut up."

He left the table, walked around in the living room, poked the fire and put some more wood on it.

"I don't want a man to love me who doesn't love me," the woman screamed.

He went into the kitchen. The woman got up from her chair and ran to the other side of the table, away from him.

"If you don't love me, get out!"

"I told you I don't want the kids to hear that screaming."

"Get out!" the woman screamed, then fell to the floor, sobbing the way that made him think of money all the time and wouldn't let him think of anything else.

He lifted the woman and held her in his arms.

"You mustn't let yourself scream that way. I *want* to love you. Why don't you let me? It's easy to let me. You don't have to do anything but be on the level and love Johnny and Rosey and not *talk* about it."

When she had stopped sobbing he walked with her to the living room and sat with her there, looking at the fire. It was a small fire now, barely a fire at all. The door of the bedroom opened and the little girl wandered out into the hall, sobbing the way her mother had just sobbed, naked and sobbing.

The woman ran to the girl and took her in her arms.

"Did you have a bad dream? It's all gone now. You don't have to cry any more. You sit on the toddy and Mama'll give you some water and then you go right back to sleep."

He heard the girl stop crying and then he heard the woman and the girl talking softly.

When the woman came back she said, "I'm afraid she heard us. I'm so ashamed."

If I had thirty thousand dollars, the man thought, I could straighten this out.

CHAPTER
16

Seven years ago, a little before he met her, he was thirty-two and free and anything could happen because he was a son, not a father, which more than anything in the world he wanted to be. But he wanted the mother of his kids to be all right, so he was taking his time.

You had to take your time, you just couldn't start your kids anywhere. You wanted them to have a mother who was all right, because once somebody was their mother she was their mother forever. You had to think about that.

Everybody knew what a difference a mother could make. If a man took his time and finally got to somebody who looked as if she'd be all right, as if she was the one for them, then the time taken would be worth it because *they* would never know about the time taken, they would only have more than they might have had if the time hadn't been taken, they'd have more because their mother had more.

You had to keep thinking about that because whatever you were yourself couldn't be helped, but whatever their mother would be for them *could* be. You could see that she would be the best you could find for them. You could keep looking.

Besides being fun, looking was important for the kids. You wanted several of them, not two or three but six or seven, or eight or nine. If their mother was all right, why not a lot of them? They might enjoy it. It might just turn out that they might be very happy about it, happy about their mother, their father, one another, and everybody else.

It was lonely enough waiting to see them, but it was better to go on being lonely than to see them unhappy about it, not caring about it, not enjoying it, not glad and nicely made inside and out. It was lonely most of the time, but you had to hold out, you had to keep looking, you had to keep guessing what they would be apt to be like with one and then with another and if they wouldn't be apt to be enough, you had to wait some more.

Whoever they were to be, they were entitled to the best mother their father could find, because they were stuck with him. He was the only father they'd ever have. It was him or nobody at all.

There was the actress who had been famous but wasn't any more and was drinking all the time because she wasn't but said she could have a lot of them, surely three, she had started acting when she was just a kid, she was thirty but thirty wasn't so much. (Dubious.) She had something for them: but she couldn't get to sleep unless she was drunk or took sleeping pills and she looked bad until five in the afternoon and seemed to be trembling a little all the time until then. That might not be so good for them. She had plenty, though: she was deeply funny and clean and had an innocence you had to love, for she had had affairs with half a dozen known playboys and surely half a dozen unknown ones. She was slim, too, and had a way of talking you couldn't resist because although it wasn't natural, although it had been cultivated and frequently disappeared, was very pleasing to the ear, her voice rising sweetly in the right places in a manner so artificial as to be refreshing.

There was the girl who had studied ballet since childhood but had learned to do other dancing because she had to live and danced almost naked in night clubs and said, "It's so humiliating when they're rude, when they say things. One

74

night at the beginning of my number I was slapped on the buttocks [Refined] and didn't even stop, but after the number I sat down and cried." She was well made and had a pleasant nature. She was shy and serious-minded and laughed when she was happy, and didn't want to dance for a living. She was afraid of having them, though. It wasn't just a small fear that would go away. She was afraid because her mother had died when she had been four years old, when her sister had been born, and she had heard her mother dying.

There was the girl who wrote delicate poetry and looked like nothing until she was seen whole and then looked very much like something white and astonishing because the rest of the time she looked bleak and dull because her face was bleak and dull and her hair dry and perhaps dirty. She talked a lot about the discipline of writing poetry. (Not interesting.) She had a nice name in the poetry world and loved to work at poetry. They were walking through the slums one day and a small girl with a dirty face and a running nose said hello to her and she didn't say hello to the girl but said, "I don't know why they have them."

There was the girl who must have been a little crazy, who got past the desk at the hotel and climbed thirty flights of stairs because the elevator boys would have stopped her: rang his doorbell and when he opened the door walked in quickly unbuttoning her dress at the front and saying, "I've got to take a shower first because I had to walk up." The reason he gave some thought to her in relation to them was that she came from peasants—they had been wine-makers in the old country. Her feet were fine to see, although dark and a little rough, for she had never paid much attention to herself. She had thick black hair and the whitest teeth he had ever seen in anyone who wasn't black. She was the third from the last in a family of eleven children, and her parents had always been poor but had always managed to get a great deal of food onto the table for everybody to eat, and wine. Even if she had been the one, it wouldn't have done, though, for she only wanted to go on the stage. She came back a second time, taking the stairs, so he let it be known that she was to be permitted to ride the elevators. She was grateful for this and said, "You didn't have to do that." (Never forget her.)

There was the woman who said she was the feature writer for a newspaper in South Carolina and wanted an interview but didn't ask any questions and seemed to be under the impression that he was the man who had written a book another writer had written.

There was the woman who did publicity for a famous night club and was all right until one night she said, "Let me do your publicity."

There were others and they were all just fine for him but not for them. They were right for the time, but not for afterwards.

Well, now it *was* afterwards. He was no longer a son, and there was his poor woman, there was their mother, sitting before the fire in despair, biting the fingernails that she had had manicured a few hours ago.

CHAPTER
17

He was standing at the window watching the cars and street-
cars go by. They hadn't spoken for five minutes because
they'd had another fight.

They had a fight every day, but every six or seven days they
had a big one, and then the woman screamed or the man beat
her. They had them all the time. The bad ones were very bad.
They felt ashamed and hopeless, and the only thing that
started them out again was the kids, remembering them or
having to take care of them, the way the woman had just
taken care of the crying girl.

The man wanted to say something that would be true and
helpful, but no matter what he said after a fight nothing happened, and the next day there was another fight. After six or
seven days there was another big one.

He had already told her how they could be all right, but
he had told her that during or after almost every fight they
had ever had, except the little ones. Couldn't he just let her
be? Couldn't he ask no more of her and go along with *her*
rather than ask her to go along with him?

He could.

And he would if he didn't have to write.

That's what it came to.

If he could get hold of thirty thousand dollars and count on an income of twenty-five thousand a year, that would do it. She wouldn't have to change at all. He would go along with her and be glad to forget writing.

Why not?

All he had ever wanted was a family. The reason he had written in the first place was to be able to have a family. They could have more kids, and let the other writers do the writing.

The trouble was you had to have money to have more kids, too, and there was no way for him to get money except by writing.

"I think this may straighten us out," he said at last. "Once a year I'll go off for a month and write a book. The rest of the year we'll have money. If I work hard and have a little luck, I think it'll work."

The woman didn't speak. She didn't even turn.

"What I'm thinking," he said, "is this. During that month you'll have a chance to think about a lot of things for yourself and I'll have nothing else to think about except the writing I want to do. The month will be gone before we know it and the rest of the year will be all ours."

"I mean," he said, "I'll have the book and the advance on it. And after it's published it'll earn enough for a year. If it turns out to be something Hollywood wants, we'll earn enough for *more* than a year."

Still the woman didn't speak. The man turned away to look out the window again.

I wish I knew what to tell her, he thought.

"Go now," the woman said. She wasn't excited. She was just tired and angry.

The man turned but the woman was still looking at the fire.

"If you're so anxious to get away from me, go now."

"I was thinking we'd make arrangements first."

"I know you're sick of me, so go now. Tonight."

"I thought we might plan it, start the first of next month.

78

That would give us a couple of weeks to get everything organized and I could be thinking about the writing, so that once I got there I could get straight to work and not waste a week or two."

"If you weren't sick of me, you could write upstairs. Other writers are married."

"I don't know how they do it. Maybe some of them go off a month or two."

"You can go off for a month or two, too. You can go off for a year. Think how much you could write in a year. You can go off forever. You could write *everything* then."

"What's the use making things more difficult?"

"Yes, what's the use?"

"I thought you might understand."

"Well, I don't."

"Let's forget it, then."

"Why should you forget it? You want to go off and write, so go ahead. Why forget it?"

"I wouldn't be able to write if I went off this way. I'd be too worried about you and the kids."

"Don't worry about us. You just get up and go and write."

The woman got up and went to the bedroom.

I've got to figure out a way to get work done upstairs, he thought.

He went to the bedroom and sat on his bed.

"I'll tell you what. I'll work upstairs. I'll get up in the morning and get the kids going so you can sleep until you're rested, but once I get upstairs, let me stay there until I'm through for the day. That ought to be around five. Maybe six. Once in a while maybe seven. But I'll be up there all the time. I won't come down for lunch. I'll take some stuff up there and put it in the refrigerator and get anything I want any time I want it. I won't see so much of the kids, but that'll be better for them. I'm seeing too much of them. It won't be so bad. I don't want to go off for a month. It's too lonesome, too expensive, and I've got a whole flat upstairs to work in. All I've got to do is get the place organized a little,

79

get the decks cleared for work, and make up my mind to keep a schedule the same as any other working man. We'll keep the gate locked so that nobody can ring the doorbell. You'll know nobody can get in, so you won't feel scared. This place is perfect for work if I'd only get things organized a little. If you take the kids for a walk, lock the gate after you. On Sundays we'll take them for a drive and have a picnic somewhere. I won't work on Sundays, just the weekdays from ten to about five or six. At night we'll listen to the radio and dance or talk or read. First thing you know you'll be pregnant again and I'll be working and we'll be getting money. I mean, we'll like it."

"Are you sure you wouldn't rather go?"

"Yes, I am. I've got to see all of you every day."

"Not just the kids? Me, too?"

"Yes, you, too. We'll plan it, the same as if I was going away. Tomorrow you go and see your friends, but the next day we'll go to work planning it, getting things straightened out and organized. We'll both have to work hard for three or four days getting things ready. I'll help you down here and take care of upstairs because once we get started, we've got to keep going. You've got to have things all in order down here so you won't get too tired keeping things going. Once everything's organized and you know what you're doing, it won't be hard, it'll be fun."

"I'm sorry about what happened tonight. Are you?"

"Yes, I am."

The woman ran to him and he embraced her tenderly, because they were both so pathetic and helpless.

CHAPTER
18

The woman came back from the kids' room and said, "They're both fast asleep. It's only ten o'clock. Couldn't we telephone somebody to come over?"

"Is Rosey all right?"

"Sound asleep."

"Has she got it stuck up?"

"No. She's sprawled. Come and see."

They went and saw the girl lying on her back, sprawled, relaxed and naked. The woman pointed to the part that made the child a woman and laughed softly because it was so pretty. The boy was sprawled face down, his arms out, his hands loose, his face dark and serious and unwinking.

The man turned from the boy and took the woman in his arms and held her.

"They're good kids. They're both good kids. Better than we deserve."

He held her head in his hands now to tell her he loved her. He said the words with embarrassment and hope, wanting to say them with more than his voice and mouth, wanting to say them with all of his life, even if he had to try to do it in the only language she understood, the absurd language of movie and play, novel and story, the meaningless language of the

81

glib mouth, the glib heart and head and emotion, but hopeful that she would know what he meant, hopeful that she would get it, it ought to be easy to get, why couldn't she get it? You *live* love, you don't talk it, you live it every minute, you work at it, you never let it get away, you live it because there's no other decent way to live. The saying of the words embarrassed him, for they stank, they lied, they had always lied, they oversimplified, they made a gag out of the only decent way to stay alive, loving, no matter what, loving in spite of the lies, in spite of the truth, in spite of the ugliness, in spite of the hatred, in spite of the madness, the damned unbalance, the incalculable difference, the alienations, the irresponsibilities, the malicious mischief, the arrogance, the scheming, the pretending, the deceiving.

He tried to tell her for the first time since they had met that it was so, hoping she would get it, not hear the words they had kicked around so much, but get it, know it, understand it, let it reach her. He looked into her eyes in nakedness and humility, then kissed her on the mouth, softly at first, to be the kissing of all of him, everything he was, and then slowly with pleasure, with passion, with lust, to be the kissing of his body. Her mouth was dry and sick at first, sick because she had had such a rough time, but after a moment it sweetened and seemed to smell and taste of milk, the milk of herself at peace, and glad. He loved that, and would not leave it, for he wanted her to be at peace, and glad, always, not just when it was like this, but all the time.

"Let's sit down and drink," the woman said.

"Sure."

They sat at the table in the kitchen and began to drink.

"I'm so excited. That's why I want to drink. I want to get drunk. You get drunk, too."

"Sure."

"I'm going to have so much fun seeing them tomorrow."

For a moment the man believed she meant the kids, but then he remembered her friends and knew she meant them.

He swallowed everything in his glass and poured more over the ice.

"Was that straight?"

"Yes."

"Let's get really pissed."

"Sure."

"I like you best when you're really gone."

"Here's to you, always."

"You're so attractive when you're gone. Shall we telephone somebody to come over?"

"Who?"

"Ellen and Charley?"

"They were here last night."

"Who, then?"

"I don't know. I'd just as soon not see anybody, but if you can think of somebody, call them."

"I could look in my book."

"O.K."

The woman fetched her book and began to read the names in alphabetical order. They were people who were mainly in New York and Hollywood. Every time she came to a name of somebody in San Francisco, it was somebody like Ellen and Charley, and the woman held her nose. He didn't blame her much, either, because they weren't very interesting. They were people they had met accidentally at the Top of the Mark, or at Vanessi's, or at The Fairmont, or at one or another of the places people in San Francisco go to when they want to celebrate, as they put it. The other people, the ones in New York and Hollywood, were mainly famous people, but they weren't very interesting, either. They were less interesting than the people in San Francisco, as a matter of fact. Some of them were a little on the monstrous side, too.

She came to the name of a man who had been a villain in the movies for thirty years but was lately more or less retired, devoting himself to his fifth wife, a girl thirty years younger than himself, and their adopted son and daughter.

"You like them, don't you?" the woman said.

"I don't mind them."

"We had such fun with them when we were in New York. They're such fun and they admire you so much. Why don't we call them and tell them to fly up for a drink? They're not far from Burbank and the planes leave every hour. They'd be here at one or two and we could drink until four or five. They could sleep upstairs or go to a hotel. You could drive to the airport and bring them here. I won't be afraid. The gate's locked. Let me call them."

"O.K."

The woman brought the telephone from the hall into the kitchen and set it down in front of her on the table. After a moment she was talking to the girl. It seemed that the retired villain was tired, but it also seemed that his wife might be able to win him over to the idea.

"She's asking him. I *do* hope they'll do it. It'll be such fun and we've got three more bottles of Scotch."

The retired villain didn't think he was up to it, so then the woman mentioned that her friends in New York were flying in in the morning and they could all meet for lunch and shopping and cocktails, then dinner and a lot of drinking and talking somewhere. The wife of the retired villain took the matter up with him again, and then she said they'd telephone the airport and a hotel in San Francisco and call right back.

"They'll come," the woman said. "I know they will. I'll wear my new dress and you shave and put on your dark suit. Don't get too drunk to drive to the airport. Maybe you'd better start shaving now, so I can get in there and bathe. We'll start drinking when they get here."

"O.K."

He finished his third drink and went into the bathroom to shave. He was in the shower when the woman said, "They're coming. They'll be at the airport at one fifteen. If they miss that plane, they'll be there at two fifteen. Now hurry, so I can get in there."

"O.K."

CHAPTER
19

He was driving to the airport to get them, shaved, in his dark suit, and just beginning to feel the three drinks he'd had before the shower and the two after. He felt pretty good.

The way I'll do it is this, he said, almost out loud. I've got the money I won this afternoon. I'll bet half of it back tomorrow. If I lose, I'll bet the rest of it back. If I win, I'll stop for the day. The next day I'll do the same. I think I'll win. All I've got to do is guess right. I ought to be able to guess right. I'll bet them across the board, so if I don't guess *exactly* right, I'll still win, or break even. I was always lucky and I'll be lucky tomorrow, and the day after tomorrow, too. I'll never stop being lucky. I always liked to write but I didn't like it any more than I liked having fun. I know I ought to work harder, but why should I? I don't feel like it. A lot of the boys who work harder but aren't lucky don't do as well as I do. They just work harder and get less because they're not lucky. Most of them show it, too. They look like hell and you know they feel worse. They never have any real fun, either. They never have the time or energy to have any. They get serious about their work when they aren't lucky and they get old fast and die without *ever* having any real fun. What for? So a handful of critics who aren't lucky and probably never took a chance on anything in their lives can sit down and say their writing stinks? Not that it doesn't. What else could it do, written by writers who aren't lucky, who never took a chance on anything? It stinks all right, but they worked hard at it, hoping it wouldn't stink, or maybe that it would stink so badly somebody would invent a new scheme of measurement and come to the conclusion that because it stinks so badly it *is* great. A writer who isn't lucky can probably find comfort in thinking like that. Maybe the stuff will be so ungame, so dull, so tiresome, so hopeless as to be great. Any unlucky writer can ask, What's greatness? And answer to suit himself. I'm lucky, though, and I don't have to do that. All I've got to do is stop worrying about the kids. They're hers and they're mine and worrying isn't going to do them any good. All worry can do is spoil my luck. It's been spoiling it for seven years as it is, but it's not too late. All I've got to do is stop worrying. Forget the kids. Forget the writing. Forget the marriage. Forget the other kids I want. I'll have them soon enough if I stop worrying. Forget the fights. Forget everything and just be lucky. Just look at the entries, telephone Leo, make the bet, win and collect. I can't expect Daisy to go along the way the wives of the writers who *aren't* lucky do. Why should she? She's a beautiful girl who knows by instinct what's important and what's not. She knows by instinct what's phony. Why should she try to live the way the wives of the unlucky writers do? They sit on floors and sip sherry and talk. Their husbands are always tired from overworking their small energies. Their kids have got to be psychoanalyzed before they're nine. I'll go along with Daisy. I'll let her be. I'll let everything be. I'll stop worrying and get my luck back. I got some of it back today even though I was worrying at the time. I got it back, though. I can't get along without my luck. The only way I can get it back is not to worry.

He found a place to park, went to the airport bar, gulped

down half his drink and laughed, the way he had laughed when he had had his luck and never needed to *believe* in it.

"Sierra Fox," he said to the bartender. "Is Sierra Fox running tomorrow at Bay Meadows?"

"I'll see," the bartender said.

"Third race, I think."

He remembered the horse and liked the picture its name made: a fox in the Sierras, alone and laughing. He guessed that if it would be in *any* race it would be the third: no reason.

"I don't see it anywhere."

"Well, if he were running, and if it turned out that he was running in the third, I'd bet him. I'd bet him if it turned out that he was running in the first or fifth, too, but not so much."

"What distance?"

"Any distance. Is that the one-fifteen coming in from Hollywood out there?"

"Yes, I think it is."

"Give me one more quick one, then, please."

He gulped the second drink down and went out. He saw them and went to meet them, laughing lucky.

They looked fine, and they said they had never seen him looking better.

"Wait till you see the kids," he said, and then although he was still laughing that way there was a congestion of agony in his soul and he thought he might puke. He didn't stop laughing, though, and didn't let them stop, either. They laughed almost all the way back because everything was actually that funny: appearances, voices, words.

And then they were there, home.

CHAPTER
20

The retired villain was past sixty and heavy now instead of lean and hard the way he had been when he had been most famous and had leered at and handled some of the most beautiful women in the movies.

"I was always meant to be fat," he said. "It was just that I was so determined to be famous."

"Oh you're not fat," the woman said. "Is he?" she said to the villain's wife. "You know best."

The actor's wife said, "He's fat and I love it. What's more, *I'm* fat, too."

"You're not at all. I'm the one who's fat. You're just voluptuous. Isn't she just voluptuous, darling?"

"What?" the man said. He'd been thinking about Sierra Fox, loping up the slope, alone and laughing. He was feeling no pain and was glad they'd come up. They were just about the nicest people in the world.

"Alice," the woman said to her husband. "Alice Murphy, from hunger, no background, who married Oscar Bard for his money. I just said, 'Doesn't she look horrible?' "

"Oh Daisy, you'll never change," Alice said. "You're just jealous because I live in Hollywood and have famous people to my house every day. Just because I've got better clothes than you have. But don't worry, I've made up my mind to be more thoughtful of the needy from now on, and I'm going to send you one of my old things, a Christian Dior that I wore once. I never wear any of them more than once unless poor Oscar can't get romantic unless I wear a certain dress, and then of course I wear it in the morning, I wear it at lunch, I wear it in the evening, and I wear it to bed. Don't I, darling?"

"You've got two dresses," the villain said, "both of them bought at May's in Los Angeles, not counting whatever the hell that was you had in your suitcase when you came to live with me. I suppose some of those rags were *supposed* to be dresses."

They were all smiling or laughing all the time, drinking and talking and making fun of themselves because that's the best thing for the soul there is.

"They were dresses I inherited from my mother," Alice said. "You know my mother, darling. Remember when she telephoned and said, 'Mr. Bard, I'd like to speak to my daughter if you don't mind. I understand she's studying acting with you. She's nineteen years old, you know.' You remember Mama, don't you, darling?"

"Well, between the two of you," Oscar said, "you made it. You must have planned the whole thing very carefully. Otherwise how did she know where you were? How did she get my unlisted number? But the joke's on you, because I couldn't have been more delighted. I mean, to have you move in with me and be bored to death for five, ten, maybe fifteen years."

"What do you mean?" Alice said. And then imitated her mother: *"If you don't mind."*

She and Daisy laughed about this a long time.

The man saw the fox stop and turn, and then lope on. The villain chuckled because the joke *was* on her, it *was* on her mother, and not on him. To be past sixty and nothing much (you had to know you weren't much) and to have a luscious piece like that fall into your bed wasn't anything like what you could call bad luck.

"Five, ten, maybe fifteen years?" Alice went on. "Five, ten, fifteen years until *what*. Divorce? Are you planning to unload me when I'm old? Is that it? Well, I'm not going to *let* you unload me. I've got so much on you already, you'll never be able to unload me."

"You look absolutely gorgeous," the woman said to Alice. "Doesn't she, darling?"

"Alice? She looks as if she might very well be the best piece of tail in Hollywood."

"What's the matter with New York?" Alice said.

"What's the matter with Sacramento, too?" Daisy said. She turned on the man with mock anger. "Don't you dare say she's the best."

"I said she *might* be."

"Anything like that you've got to say about anybody, say about me, and never mind the *might be* part, either."

"O.K." That Rosey—she looked just like her mother. Would she make out all right? Not bawl that way, or scream, or bite her fingernails, or wonder what to do next for fun? Telephone New York or ask a casual acquaintance in the street to come over after dinner or badger an old New York girl friend to get up in the middle of the night and drag her husband to San Francisco? Would Rosey have a little better luck than her poor mama? Her poor mama must have had very bad luck somewhere along the line. Would Rosey have to tell lies and believe they were the truth, or not care that they weren't, or would she have better luck than her poor mama?

"O.K.?" the woman said. "What the hell is that supposed to mean?"

"What I said. The best."

"You know *that's* the truth. You know *you* never had any better."

"No, I never did."

"I swear on my mother, it's all the time."

"How *is* the old bag?" Alice said.

"She still says *shite*, because it's more refined, she thinks. Remember that time you were staying with me and we'd gotten in at four in the morning and were still in bed at four in the afternoon and she came in and said it?"

" 'Shit, Mother, shit,' you said to her," Alice said. " 'It's affected to pronounce it shite. People will never know how refined you *really* are if you pronounce it that way,' you said. I'd never heard it pronounced that way before. I think she's the only person in the world who pronounces it that way. Hasn't she poisoned her husband yet?"

"Not yet. But he ought to drop dead any day now anyway."

"Is he actually ninety-two?"

"No. He just looks ninety-two. I think he's in his early eighties, though."

"And how old is your mother?" the villain said.

"Forty," the woman said.

"*That* old?" the villain laughed. "He didn't do so good. I did a lot better than he did. Sixty-two and a wife of twenty-three isn't so bad."

"Twenty-two until day after tomorrow," Alice said.

"Yes, but *you're* young, Oscar," Daisy said, "and he's old. You know how some men are. Some are young all the time and some are old from the beginning. Well, he's been old all the time. Old and ugly. She's crazy about him, though. Well, anyhow, she *says* she is. You know how people fool themselves when they're desperate. Don't people fool themselves when they're desperate, darling?"

"When they're *not*, too."

The girls laughed and the villain chuckled.

"You want some coffee maybe?" the man asked the villain.

"Hell no. I wouldn't think of spoiling this with coffee. I haven't felt so good in years. Seeing these two together does me good, that's all. I was feeling rotten when you called. Sick of myself. I get sick that way quite a lot, always have. But hell, I said, why not? It's crazy, but why the hell not? Why don't we always do things like that? I like it here. I like sitting here and drinking and talking and watching the girls. I worked like a dog all my life. What the hell for? To be famous for twenty years as a movie villain? Never met a villain in my life. Why? Do *you* want some coffee?"

"No, but I thought you might want some, and something to eat. There isn't much in the house, but there are steaks and chops any time we want them. We've got a little bread lying around, too," he said and suddenly began to roar with laughter. "I've always loved bread," he said quickly. "If I ever get rich I'm going to buy a bakery. Alice, there are steaks and chops any time you're hungry."

"Yum yum," Alice said.

"No," the villain said. "You can't mean it, darling. For God's sake, it's only half past three. Now, please don't break this up by fooling around with steaks. You know, I haven't been in a house like this in years. I mean, where *people* live. A house, not a movie set. A *home*. I'd like to buy a house like this in San Francisco and move into it myself."

"Don't do it, Oscar," the woman said. "It stinks. It's small. The front door opens right into the whole house. The living room and the hall are stuck together. This is no house."

"It's the best house I've ever been in," the villain said.

"There was nothing else new to be had when I got out of the Army," the man said. "Daisy was pregnant and we had to have something so I figured that something out by the ocean would be fine. This was out by the ocean and almost finished: they were painting it. I had a little money then, so I paid cash for it, and we moved in. It stinks all right, but it's not so bad. There's a big fenced-in yard, mostly lawn, with rose bushes and other stuff around. The kids play there. Upstairs is another apartment just like this one, and I work there. If we've got a nurse, we both live up there and the kids and the nurse live down here, and I work in the second bedroom, the one that the kids sleep in down here, but it's not like a bedroom any more, shelves all around and a desk. It's a small room to begin with and after the shelves were put in it got smaller, but it's a good place to work. I figured out by the ocean would be fine. I never cared for a place that wasn't near the ocean."

"It's the best house I've ever been in," the villain said. "My house isn't a house, it's an institution for the help. Three full-time gardeners alone. I come from the East Side in New York, so I'm living in a castle in Beverly Hills. I don't feel at home there."

"You've lived there almost thirty years," the villain's wife said. "What do you mean you don't feel at home there? Are you trying to get me to move to the East Side in New York or something?"

"I'm drunk," the villain said suddenly, "but I love it. And I'm going to get drunker. This is the kind of house I want to live in, that's all. I know I never will, but this is the kind I want to."

That's the way I'll do it, the man thought. Sierra Fox. This is too good to be cluttered with any other program. The kids are asleep. They're all right. All I've got to do is get my luck back and get the money we need.

The fox loped on up the slope, stopped and turned, alone and laughing.

CHAPTER
21

The night ended in daylight, the villain and his wife went off in a taxi to the St. Francis, and the woman said, "I told her it's all the time. What do you want to do, make a liar out of me?"

"It's after five. In a little while Rosey's going to be waking up Johnny. And if you're going to have the big day you think you are, you'd better get some sleep."

"Sleep isn't the only thing I need at night. You can get in bed and *hold* me, can't you?"

"I'm not going to bed."

"Why not?"

"I might fall asleep and not want to get up when Johnny comes in."

"He won't come in for at least an hour. Please take off your clothes and get in bed."

The man stretched out on her bed without taking off his shoes, even. The woman was under the covers and he bundled her up in them and held her tight because she was drunk and lonely and happy and half dead.

"They're so rich," she said. "They've got so much money. Did you see that dress she was wearing? How much do you think it cost?"

"Five thousand dollars."

"It cost a thousand. She told me. But she didn't look as beautiful as I did, did she?"

"No."

"Don't just say it."

"No, you looked best. You became a little prettier each time you had a kid. She hasn't had any."

"That isn't it. I'm more beautiful anyway."

"Yes, you are."

"But she *is* fun. Lucretia isn't fun the way Alice is. Lucretia's a dope compared to Alice but much more beautiful. Don't you think Lucretia's much more beautiful than Alice?"

"I guess so."

Actually they all looked about the same: that is, young and pretty.

"Is Lucretia more beautiful than I am?"

"I don't think so."

"Don't you *know*?"

"No, she's not."

He'd been through this routine too many times not to know that even dead-tired she'd be miserable if he didn't agree with everything. She'd start an argument that would go on for hours, sometimes days. It was *still* going on. This was part of it because long ago, years ago, he had tried to tell her something about beauty, that it came from inside, and a woman who was plain on the outside could very well be beautiful because she was beautiful inside. She hadn't ever been beautiful that way, not even after Johnny was born, not even after Rosey was. It was only when she bawled that she was anything at all inside, but it wasn't beautiful, it was pathetic.

"Would you like to lay Lucretia?"

"No."

"You probably would, but don't you dare make a pass at her. I'd be so humiliated I'd never be able to speak to her again. After the things I've told her about how you adore me. You won't make a pass at her, will you?"

"No."

"Not even the littlest kind of pass? You know. Don't look at her the way you do sometimes. Just be nice to her, but don't look at her that way. You looked at Ellen Flesch that way last night. I didn't make anything of it because she's Ellen, but it would be awful if it was Lucretia."

"I'll just open my eyes a little when it's Lucretia."

"No, don't be funny. This is serious. Alice and Lucretia are my best friends. Alice is O.K. because she's really in love with her husband, and I know you're O.K. as far as she's concerned because you didn't look at her once that way all night. But Lucretia isn't in love with her husband. She *says* she is, she *thinks* she is, but I know she isn't, and all she'd need to make my life hopeless would be one little pass from you. So you won't, will you?"

"No."

"Do you love me?"

"Yes."

"With all your heart?"

"Yes."

"Am I the most beautiful girl in the world?"

"Yes."

"Am I the best wife a man could ever have and the best mother and the best lay and the most intelligent and the most inspiring girl?"

"Yes."

"That's nice."

She giggled at her joke, turned quickly to be kissed, and then fell asleep.

The man held her a moment, then got up, covered her, made the room as dark as possible, went out and closed the door.

He stood at the door of the children's room and listened. Rosey was saying half-asleep things. He went to the bathroom, shaved, showered and dressed, put coffee on, fetched the morning paper and sat down at the kitchen table to have a look at the entries.

Sierra Fox wasn't running.

The sixth looked best. They were Makai, Sunfair, Pay Me, Cold Roll, Court Toubo, Hail Victory, Valdina Andire, and Cyclone. He would telephone Leo around half past three and bet two hundred across on Pay Me at four to one. Post time would be about four, the race would be over by four fifteen, but he wouldn't bother to find out who got it. He'd forget he'd made the bet. He had the money for it and more besides, enough for two more bets of the same size. He put the paper aside because he didn't want to be tempted to change his hunch. It was a good one. Six hundred dollars on Pay Me to win, place, and show.

The matter of money was off his mind for the rest of the day.

The boy came out and stood in the kitchen doorway, yawning, stretching and smiling.

"I smell coffee."

"I'm making some."

"Papa, why can't little boys—why can't *big* boys drink coffee?"

"You can drink coffee."

"I can't."

"You can have a little this morning."

"How much?"

"As much as you like."

"I can't, can I?"

"Yes, you can have coffee. Coffee's all right. I'll fix you a cup. Is Rosey awake?"

"A little. She's saying funny words."

"Do you want to sleep some more?"

"Sleep some *more?* I want to get dressed. I want to drink coffee. Can I sit at the big table with you?"

"Sure. Let's be quiet, though, so Rosey can sleep some more."

"She's not sleeping. She's saying poopoo and paypay and things like that."

He dressed the boy, then the girl, they had breakfast together at the big table, and then he turned them loose in the yard.

Pay Me in the sixth.

CHAPTER
22

The woman was up at noon needing coffee. She made telephone calls while she had coffee and got the day organized. The three couples would meet at two o'clock at the St. Francis for lunch. After that the girls would go shopping and the boys would either go with them or sit somewhere and drink and talk. At six they'd all go home and rest and change and meet again at nine for dinner somewhere. After that they'd think of something else.

"What about the kids?" the man said.

"I thought you'd telephone Marta. She could spend the night. We could sleep upstairs or maybe at a hotel. Wouldn't it be fun at a hotel?"

"I thought you never wanted Marta to step into this house again."

"Well, who could we get? After all, she's in the family. She's something to the kids. We couldn't feel so relaxed about the kids with anybody else. I hate her, but who else could we get?"

"I'll stay with the kids. You go ahead. After dinner tonight if you feel like it bring them out. I'll buy some more Scotch and some stuff to eat."

"Why should you stay with the kids? Let Marta come and stay with them."

"We've treated her pretty badly."

"Well, call her anyway. There's nobody else."

"I'll stay."

"I told them we'd *all* meet. *I'll* call Marta."

The woman called her and then said, "I must say she was delighted about the whole idea, but why shouldn't she be? She ought to feel lucky to have a chance to be near two kids like Johnny and Rosey. She's ready any time you are. She knows where everything is. She said she'd be glad to stay as long as we like. Maybe we could spend a couple of nights at a hotel, maybe drive somewhere afterwards for a couple of days, maybe drive Alice and Oscar home and stay with them overnight or something."

"I'll go get Marta."

"What's the matter? You're not sore, are you?"

"I'm a little tired. After Marta gets here I'm going upstairs for a nap while you're dressing."

He drove three miles to where Marta lived in a small apartment. On the way back she asked that he stop a moment at the Safeway. When she came out she was carrying a carton full of groceries. The man took the carton from her, put it in the car, and handed her a hundred dollars.

"In case we're away a couple of days. I'll telephone of course."

"All right. Is it all right if I clean the place?"

"You don't have to go to all that trouble."

"No. I like to do it. I'd like to clean both flats if it's all right."

"The top flat *does* need a little looking after, at that. You're very kind, Marta."

"Oh, don't talk silly, please."

The woman ran in her negligee that you could see through and embraced and kissed Marta, the way she always did, friend and enemy alike, and the man went upstairs.

He wanted to get it off his mind, so he telephoned Leo

and said, "Put me down for two hundred across on Pay Me in the sixth."

That was it. That was all there was to it. If Pay Me won he'd know he was getting his luck back and that he'd soon have everything straightened out.

He stretched out on the davenport in the living room, which was his workroom whenever they lived downstairs. He worked at a bridge table. The other room, the original workroom, was too small. He felt trapped in that room.

When the woman woke him up he remembered that he had been dreaming about the fox.

"How do I look?" she said.

"You look fine. Is that a pimple on your chin?"

"Isn't it *hidden?*" She opened her handbag and looked into the small mirror at the pimple. "Well, it's a very beautiful pimple. Isn't it?"

"What?" the man said. He was still half asleep and trying to remember more about the fox.

"Isn't it? The pimple. Beautiful?"

"Oh," the man said. "Yes, it is."

The woman giggled because she knew how tiresome it was to make him answer all the silly questions she just somehow couldn't help asking. He knew she couldn't, but he wished to God she'd lay off some day. He got up.

"Do you have any money?" the woman said. "I mean, they're all so rich, but we've got to pay for things just the same because they're visiting us."

"I've got some."

"Not twenty or thirty dollars. You ought to have at least a hundred and fifty or so, and I ought to have fifty at least. We'd better stop at the bank."

"I was there yesterday," the man said.

He took fifty out of his wallet and handed it to the woman.

"How much do we have left?"

"The account's still open."

"What are we going to do?"

"I ought to be getting some money from England pretty soon. It's all right."

"Are you sure?"

"Come on, let's go."

If Pay Me came in he'd pick up the money and deposit it and tell her the money from England had come. He'd keep the rest in cash.

They began to drive to town.

"You won't make a pass at Lucretia, will you?"

"I don't like her. I like her less than I like Alice. Why would I make a pass at her?"

"I thought you liked Alice. I thought you liked Lucretia, too."

"I don't mind them because they're your friends, that's all."

"Well, don't make a pass at her, anyway. All right?"

"All right."

"We'll have fun, won't we?"

"I've been having fun ever since I got out of the Army."

"There's plenty of time for your writing. Three years in the Army for a man like you isn't something you can get over just like that. You need time."

"I've had three years."

"It isn't as if you had been a colonel or something. You were a private. You need fun after three years of that. We'll have a lot of fun. Is the pimple awful?"

"Nobody'll notice it."

"I'm starved. We'll order everything. All right?"

"Sure. I want some onion soup and a steak. I'm a little hung over."

"Lucretia's afraid of you."

"I'd rather not hear about it."

"She told me so. She thinks you're mysterious."

"Shit."

"She's jealous of me, but she was being honest when she told me she was afraid of you. She was sorry she said it, but I nagged at her and made her tell me everything. It was when they came out to dinner when we were in Long Island. She said when you look at her she feels gooey all over."

"Shut up."

"That's why you've got to look at *me* all the time."

The car stopped at a red light and the man turned to look at the woman.

"Lay off a little, will you? I'm kind of tired."

The woman giggled, then pressed beside him.

"I love you so much," she said.

The light changed and they moved on.

Pay Me. That was it. Pay me because I need it badly. Pay me because my wife's nuts and I want to see if I can help her. Pay me because she can't help herself. Pay me because she's driving me nuts too and I don't want to do any of the things I keep stopping myself from doing. Pay me so I can get this thing worked out. Pay me so I can have enough money to be able to forget all about it and see if I can help this girl who's Johnny's and Rosey's mother and my wife. Pay me so I can see about getting back to my work. Pay me, that's all.

CHAPTER
23

It was half past two in the afternoon when they reached the hotel lobby, but no one was around, so the woman telephoned Lucretia. Her voice was high and excited when she began to speak, but it became swiftly hushed. (They couldn't have lunch, most likely.)

"Something terrible's happened," the woman said.

She brought out the small bottle of smelling salts she always carried around in her handbag, unscrewed the top, and waved the open neck of the small bottle in front of her nose several times.

"Leander's had a heart attack. A bad one. They took him to the hospital an hour ago. He's not expected to live. That was Alice. She's alone up there and scared to death. She and Oscar saw it happen. Oscar went along with Lucretia, and Alice stayed up there to wait for phone calls from Oscar. I guess we'd better go up."

"How about a drink at the bar first?"

"I *need* one, but she's waiting. I told her I'd be right up."

"You go up. I'll have a drink and be up in a moment."

"It's room eleven oh seven."

She threw her arms around the man and hugged him desperately.

"It couldn't happen to you, could it?" she said.

She giggled a little, then said, "It wouldn't *dare.*"

But when he saw her face there were tears in her eyes.

"I feel so sorry for Lucretia," she said.

"*She* didn't have the attack."

"How could she have the attack? She's twenty-three. Don't take too long and don't look at anybody."

She went off as if to a party that promised to be the best yet. The man went to the mezzanine bar instead of to the Men's Bar which he knew would be full of the more successful of the town's businessmen and he didn't want to overhear any of their talk.

He had one drink quickly, expecting to go on up and listen to the details, but he decided he'd need at least one more, first. Besides, they ought to have enough time to get their real feelings about the matter out of their systems, so that by the time he got there they could pretend to be shocked and upset.

When he got up to the room he found both girls in tears.

"He's dead," the woman said. "Lucretia tried to throw herself out of the window of the hospital. It's a good thing Oscar was there."

"Oscar just phoned," Alice said. "They've given Lucretia a sedative and want her to go to bed, but she doesn't want to."

"What does she want to do?"

"Throw herself out the window," the woman said.

"What floor are they on?"

"Oh, shit," the woman said, and then both of the women who had been sobbing bitterly began to laugh.

"You dirty son of a bitch, you," the woman said.

"What are you laughing about?" the man said.

"We'd better not be laughing when we see Lucretia and Oscar," Alice laughed. "Lucretia's got her chance to suffer at last and Oscar's scared to death of heart attacks. All his friends have had them."

"What about lunch?"

"Lunch?" the woman laughed. "How can you talk about

lunch at a time like this? We've got to stay here until Oscar phones again."

"He's been stuttering like mad," Alice said, trying not to laugh. "I never heard him stutter before. He wanted to know if he should telephone the Associated Press, and he kept asking if I knew who Leander's mother is. He thinks everybody's got a mother."

"I'd hate to be hanging since Leander had a mother," the woman said. "He was almost seventy, wasn't he?"

"Well, whatever he was," Alice said, "his mother would be at least a hundred if she were alive."

"What's the schedule now? I'd like to get some lunch."

"Don't leave us," Alice said. "Have lunch up here. I'll call room service. What do you want?"

"Onion soup and a sirloin, rare, but I don't want to eat up here. They may be coming back in a little while."

"I'm going to eat, too," Alice said. "I'm starved. They won't be back for hours. This is Lucretia's big chance. And by the time Oscar gets through calling the Associated Press and L. B. Mayer and his own mother in New York it'll be early evening."

"Well, order for me, too, then," Daisy said. "I'll have the same, but I'd like a real nice dessert, too. We'll pay for it."

The villain's wife ordered lunch and when it came the man's wife paid for it and tipped the waiter and waited for him to step respectfully out of the room in which the celebrated Leander Asp had had a heart attack. Then she began to laugh again.

"He didn't notice that we've been laughing, did he?" Alice said. "Lucretia would never forgive us if she found out."

"He doesn't know anything about it," the man said. "They all walk that way at the hotels where the rates are high. How much was the bill?"

"Forty."

"The hell it was."

"Well, I want forty anyway," the woman said.

The man gave her forty, they sat down, and began to eat.

After lunch the man stretched out on one of the beds in the bedroom, but the woman said, "Not that one, that's the one they stretched *him* out on." The man didn't move, though, and the woman flung herself on the bed and hugged him.

"We'll be all right," she said. "We're both *young* and *healthy,* anyhow."

"You're young, and I'm healthy, but we'll be all right all right just the same."

"What are we going to do about money, though? It goes so quickly. Is there some coming from England, or did you just say that?"

"No, there's some coming. It's about due now."

He looked at his watch.

They're out on the track now, he thought, moving to the starting gate.

The villain's wife came into the room and said, "Nothing doing, you two."

The woman got up and she and Alice went into the other room. The man heard them talking softly now and not laughing any more. Valenzuela was just about the best boy at the track and he'd bring her in. His eyes closed and he fell into dreamless sleep. When he woke up the place was dark and he saw that it was after five. He reached over for the phone and heard his wife talking softly to Lucretia. It was about the funeral being day after tomorrow in San Francisco because, Lucretia said, he had always loved San Francisco. His lawyers were flying out with a lot of papers and things, and so was his secretary, Anthony. The man hung up, waited five minutes and then tried again. Leo answered the phone and the man said, "What did she pay?"

"Eleven forty, seven eighty, and four forty. I haven't figured out what it comes to yet. Will I be seeing you in a half-hour or so?"

"O.K." He hung up and fell back to sleep. When he woke up again, five minutes later, he believed he had dreamed it. He thought about it a moment and then remembered the woman talking with Lucretia, so he knew he hadn't. Valenzuela *had* brought her in. And the horse had paid better than he had expected. The place money was especially good. He got up and went into the bathroom and splashed cold water on his face.

When he stepped into the other room he was not surprised to find the women talking and sobbing softly.

"Is there anything I can do?"

"No," Alice said. "They're coming in pretty soon."

"How's Oscar?"

"He's pretty shaken up. I wish he hadn't seen it. He doesn't want to drink any more and he says he's going to see about walking more. And he wants a thorough medical examination as soon as we get home. We're staying for the funeral of course."

"How's Lucretia?"

"She's absolutely in despair," Daisy said. "I talked to her and she doesn't know what to do or where to turn. I made her promise to stay at our house after the funeral. We're going to take flowers to his grave every day."

"How long are you planning to do that?"

"Oh, for two or three days, I guess. Or at least until the photographers get through taking pictures. They've been taking them all afternoon of course, but she says she looks like hell."

"Oh, Daisy," Alice said. "He *was* a great man. He got ten thousand dollars a portrait. He painted everybody in society."

"He didn't paint my mother, and he didn't paint yours, *either*. He'd have a nice time getting ten thousand dollars out of your mother for making her look like Garbo instead of garbage."

"Oh, Daisy, I miss my mother so. Don't you?"

"I'd have a nice time trying to get fifty cents out of my mother," Daisy said, "but I guess I miss her, too. I'll be damned if I'm going to cry about that, too, though. I've already cried because my husband beat me again night before last, because I don't have any clothes and don't have any money and never have enough fun and never go anywhere, and because there's a fly in this room. But I'll be damned if I'm going to cry because I miss my mother, too. That would be going a little *too* far. What have *you* been crying about? Own up. Don't tell any dirty lies."

"Things like that, too," Alice said.

"I'm going to take a little walk," the man said. "Can I bring you anything?"

"Just money."

He picked up a late afternoon paper at the hotel newsstand and went to the Men's Bar. He found the chart for the sixth and discovered that Valenzuela had brought her in by a nose over Makai, who beat out Cold Roll by another nose. They had come down the stretch together, and then Valenzuela had pushed Pay Me out ahead of the others a few inches. Well, that made the difference. He figured out his winnings and found that it came to four thousand one hundred and twenty dollars net, so he figured it again because he hadn't expected it to be half that much. But again it came to the same amount. He had another drink and walked to Leo's and sat down at Leo's worktable.

"Forty-one twenty, right?" Leo said and brought out a roll and began to peel off of it.

He walked back to the hotel and when he went up to the room he found Lucretia and Oscar there. Oscar seemed pale, nervous and scared. Lucretia seemed thrilled.

The man noticed that his wife was watching him carefully.

"I'm awfully sorry, Lucretia," he said.

Lucretia fell on his shoulder and began to sob, but there was only a moment of it, and then she began to walk around excitedly, talking softly to Daisy and to Alice about what a great man she had had the honor to be the wife of, as she put it, for twenty-two and a half months.

The man was glad he hadn't had to see him alive again, though, because he was so much more attractive dead, and made so many people so much more truly happy. His only real mourner was the retired villain, but of course he was in mourning for himself. He'd probably try to get out of staying on for the funeral in order to get home and have the medical check-up.

CHAPTER
24

"You've all got to have dinner," Lucretia said, "but of course I can't eat. I won't be able to eat for days. I'm absolutely sick with grief. Do you know what I think? I think it isn't true. He was so alive until the moment it happened I just can't *believe* it happened. I *won't* believe it happened. I keep thinking he's going to walk in here in the handsome way he always did and say in his wonderful voice, 'Here I am, Peaches.' That was his name for me from the beginning, from before we were married, even. Poor Leander, where are you now, my darling, my poor wonderful darling?"

She flung herself on the retired villain, who tried to comfort her without making his wife angry. He glanced at his wife fretfully, but the widow didn't stay with him too long. Something more had occurred to her to say that might seem unique and original for one in mourning.

"He was the *youngest* man I ever knew. There wasn't an old thought in his head. There simply *wasn't* an old thought in his head. There wasn't an old emotion in his," she hesitated a moment trying to guess where emotions might be said to be, and then settled for, "body, his wonderful young body."

"Oh, Lucretia," Alice said. "We couldn't eat."

"You must, you must," Lucretia sobbed. "You mustn't mind me. I'll be this way for days. I'm absolutely desolated. Please let me order for you. Oscar darling, I can't make sense over the telephone. Please order for everybody."

The villain tried to make asking everybody what they wanted to eat a thing of mourning but they kept saying rare sirloin with lyonnaise potatoes and a green salad (that was the woman getting back at Lucretia for going too far with the performing), or roast beef rare with a baked potato, and a lobster cocktail first, though.

"Yes, darling," Lucretia screamed and wept at the villain's wife. "A lobster cocktail first. Daisy? A lobster cocktail first?"

"All right."

"Do you love lobster, too?" Lucretia wept. "I could live on lobster. My poor Leander, if you were only here, we'd *all* eat lobster. He loved lobster. Dick? Lobster cocktail first?"

"O.K."

The villain went to the telephone and had a rough time stuttering the order.

During dinner the widow walked about, reminiscing (as she said) and watching the others. At last Daisy forced her to sit at the table, and then to have just a taste of the lobster, and then just a taste of the roast beef, and then just a taste of the green salad. The widow had tastes for a while, and then a plate was made for her, and she settled down to just chewing her food sadly but with relish. She didn't try anything fancy in her manner of drinking coffee, though, and just drank it like a healthy factory girl at lunch.

After dinner a thought occurred to her that she felt no one should dare resist: room service should bring up a bucket of ice, two glasses, and a bottle of Scotch for the boys, and a bottle of champagne for the girls, but of course nothing for her. No one resisted this idea and when the stuff came, the villain said he would have one drink in memory of Leander Asp. But Daisy and Alice didn't attach any strings to their drinking of the champagne and soon finished the whole bottle, so that by the time Lucretia began to be adequately coaxed

111

there was only Scotch, which she accepted and drank with a mixture of unbearable unhappiness and pleasure.

By one in the morning the girls were all drunk and talking honestly. The villain was sober, exhausted and frightened. He wanted to get to his room and bed, but he didn't dare bring the matter up. He didn't know what to make of their talk, either.

The man wasn't sure he didn't admire the manner in which the widow was mourning, but that, he knew, may have been because Pay Me had come in and because he had so much money now.

"How about some sleep?" the man said, more for the villain than for himself.

"Oh, not yet!" Lucretia said. "I'll be this way for days. I'll sleep out here on this sofa, but of course I won't sleep. And Daisy and you can sleep in the bedroom, but not yet. Don't stop now. I want to drink myself into insensibility. I must. Otherwise I don't know what I'll do."

"Maybe it would be better if just Daisy and Alice stayed with you tonight. Oscar's in the hotel, and I could go home."

"Yes," the villain said. "I'm just down the hall." He got to his feet.

"Oh, not yet, Oscar, *please*," the widow said. "Please drink again to the memory of Leander."

"I've got to take it easy on that stuff," Oscar said. "Did he like it?"

"Never touched it," the widow said. "Just wines. He *cooked* with wines. We often had it at breakfast. I've been drinking different kinds of wines for twenty-two and a half months. It isn't the Scotch that does it, Oscar darling. It's—"

The words she probably had in mind were *old age.*

"*Fate,*" she said. "It's God calling home a favorite. Leander was a favorite. God called him home. I'm very religious. Oh, please drink another to Leander's memory, Oscar."

"Well, a nightcap, then."

He poured himself a small one, drank it, embraced his wife, whispered to her, said good night, and went along.

"He's scared to death," his wife said.

"What's he scared of?" the widow said.

"What happened to Leander," Alice said.

"Oh, that won't happen to *him*," the widow said. "He doesn't drink wines, does he? It's those damn wines that did it. I warned him about them, but you know how he was. Had to have his way in everything. Christ, he put curry in everything. I hate curry. What the hell's Oscar got to be scared of? He doesn't put curry in everything, does he?"

"No, but he's sixty-two just the same."

"That's got nothing to do with it. Lots of nice people are sixty-two."

The woman went to the man suddenly.

"Don't you dare leave me," she whispered.

"Well, let's go home, then. Marta's made the beds upstairs and cleaned the place. Alice can stay with Lucretia."

"We *can't* leave her at a time like this, but don't you dare get up and go. We can sleep out here on the sofa and they can sleep inside."

"Daisy, do you know why he liked curry so much?" the widow said.

"Some people like broccoli," Daisy said.

"I hate it, don't you, Dick?" the widow said.

"I don't mind it. Listen, Lucretia, I'm going to take Daisy home. We'll be out there any time you want us. You've got the upstairs phone number, haven't you?"

"Oh, Daisy," the widow said. "You can't leave me now. You wouldn't dare. If *your* husband dropped dead, you know damn well I wouldn't leave you, so why are you trying to leave me?"

"I'm sick," Daisy said. "Honest I am. I've got to go home and take care of myself. I think I'm pregnant again."

The widow leaped on Daisy and embraced her.

"Oh, darling," she said. "How wonderful. It'll be your third. Think of it. Three kids and only twenty-three. But you can take care of yourself *here*, darling. Oh, please don't go."

"Phone me when you wake up in the morning," Daisy said.

On the way home the man said, "What do you mean, take care of yourself?"

"I thought I'd take a very hot bath. We can't afford another."

"Let me decide what we can afford or can't afford. Take care of yourself, but not that way."

"Maybe I'm not pregnant. Maybe I'm just late. I've been feeling pregnant all day, though, and I *did* want to get away."

"Why?"

"*Why?* She flirted with you from the time you arrived to the time we left, that's why. Don't tell me you didn't know."

"Was that supposed to be flirting?"

"It certainly was, and you know it. Why should I have another kid for you?"

"Because you're pregnant for one thing, if you *are* pregnant. And because whether she was flirting or not has got nothing to do with it for another. I see these people because they're your friends and because you're miserable unless you can see them and give me no peace unless I see them, too. They're your friends, that is, until they drop dead, as she said."

"You encouraged her all night."

"I was *there* all night. I didn't encourage her any more than I encouraged Alice or you. I wish to God I didn't have to see any of them any more."

"Lucretia's impossible. I never saw anybody so phony."

"She's your friend. You telephoned her in New York and made her come out here. If you'd left them alone that poor bastard would probably still be alive."

"Let's drive somewhere. Let's drive all night. Let's drive to Reno. You're not drunk."

"No, I'm not drunk, but I *am* tired, and maybe you're pregnant. We're going home. You're going to bed in your bed and I'm going to bed in mine. We'll drive somewhere after you're pregnant for sure, or not, but as long as there's

114

a chance that you are, I want you to take care of yourself. I want you to stay in bed very late tomorrow. I have in mind another boy."

"What are we going to do for money?"

"I'll take care of the money. You take care of yourself."

CHAPTER
25

"Don't read," the woman said. "Turn off the light and let's talk."

"Just let me finish this."

"The whole book?"

"Just a couple more pages."

"What is it?"

"Dostoevsky telling about the time he met Turgenev."

"Who cares about that?"

"I read it twenty years ago. Dostoevsky got sore at Turgenev for hating Russia and loving Germany. I want to find out how it happened."

"Well, read it aloud, then."

"Goncharov," the man began to read, "talked incessantly about Turgenev. I kept putting off my visit to him—still, eventually I had to call. I went about noon, and found him at breakfast. I'll tell you frankly—I never really liked the man. The worst of it is that since 1857, at Wiesbaden, I've owed him 50 dollars (which even today I haven't yet paid back!). I can't stand the aristocratic and pharisaical sort of way he embraces one, and offers his cheek to be kissed. He puts on monstrous airs; but my bitterest complaint against him is his book, *Smoke*. He told me himself that the leading idea, the point at issue, in that book, is this: 'If Russia were destroyed by an earthquake and vanished from the globe, it would mean no loss to humanity—it would not even be noticed.' He declared to me that that was his fundamental view of Russia. I found him in irritable mood; it was on account of the failure of *Smoke*."

The man glanced through a page quickly and skipped most of it because it was about nihilists, atheists and religion.

"Amongst other things," he read on, "he told me that we are bound to crawl in the dust before the Germans, that there is but one universal and irrefutable way—that of civilization —and that all attempts to create an independent Russian culture are but folly and pigheadedness. He said he was writing a long article against the Russophiles and Slavophiles. I advised him to order a telescope from Paris for his better convenience. 'What do you mean?' he asked. 'The distance is somewhat great,' I replied; 'direct the telescope on Russia, and then you will be able to observe us; otherwise you can't really see anything at all.' He flew into a rage. When I saw him so angry, I said with well simulated naivete: 'Really, I should never have supposed that all the articles derogatory to your new novel could have discomposed you to this extent; by God, the thing's not worth getting so angry about. Come, spit upon it all!' 'I'm not in the least discomposed. What are you thinking of?' he answered, getting red. I interrupted him and turned the talk to personal and domestic matters. Before going away, I brought forth, as if quite casually and without any particular object, all the hatred that these three months have accumulated in me against the Germans.

"You see," the man said to the woman, "Dostoevsky had run away from Russia because of his debts and in order to see about improving his health; but he began to gamble and lose, and the more he lost the more he hated the Germans. He never remarks anywhere that if he had won—especially if he had won all that he had wanted to win, that is, enough to pay his debts so he could return to Russia—he might not hate the Germans, might in fact like them very much. It is refreshing of him to just hate them, though.

"'Do you know,'" he read on, "'what swindlers and rogues they are here? Verily, the common people are much more evil and dishonest here than they are with us; and that they are stupider there can be no doubt. You are always talking of civilization; with what has your "civilization" endowed the Germans, and wherein do they surpass us?' He turned pale (it is no exaggeration), and said: 'In speaking thus, you insult me personally. You know quite well that I have definitely settled here, that I consider myself a German and not a Russian, and am proud of it.' I answered: 'Although I have read your *Smoke,* and have just talked with you for a whole hour, I could never have imagined that you would say such a thing. Forgive me, therefore, if I have insulted you.' Then we took leave of one another very politely, and I promised myself that I would never again cross Turgenev's threshold. The next day Turgenev came at exactly ten o'clock in the morning to my abode and left his card with the landlady. But as I had told him the day before that I never saw anyone till noon, and that we usually slept till eleven, I naturally took his ten o'clock call as a hint that he doesn't wish to see any more of me. During the whole seven weeks, I saw him only once more, at the railway station. We looked at one another, but no greeting passed. The animosity with which I speak of Turgenev, and the insults we offered one another, will perhaps strike you unpleasantly. But, by God, I can no other; he offended me too deeply with his amazing views."

"Is that the end?" the woman said.

"There's a little more, but that's the part I was after."

He shut off the light and settled down in his bed.

"Did he have a *lot* of debts?"

"It must have been quite a lot. He had to get up and run away. He had to stay away a long time, too. Two or three years. And he was homesick the whole time. The question is, Wouldn't he be homesick in Russia, too? I mean what good would Russia be if after he got there again—after losing three years in Europe and all the money he could borrow—he still couldn't get hold of any money, or certainly not as much as he needed? What good would it be if he couldn't write after he got back to Russia? When he spoke of Russia he obviously meant himself and his writing, and when Turgenev spoke of Germany he meant himself and his writing. One writer felt one region and people was superior to the other because that was the region and people he had had a little luck with in his writing. He was a lousy gambler."

"Did he ever win?"

"He always won a little at first, but then the excitement would get him and he would notice that the other gamblers were betting more and winning more and he'd feel that if they could do it, he could do it, too. He pointed out to himself that they didn't need the money as badly as he did. But he never seemed to have enough to be able to win very much, and he always ended up with everything lost, writing a very long letter to a friend explaining how it had happened, asking him not to tell a soul, and begging him for a loan, generally a second or a third one, or an advance—a further advance—on a new book."

"Were the other gamblers writers, too?"

"Don't be smart. As a matter of fact, one or two of them were, but how many writers will you ever see at a gambling casino?"

"Did the other writer, the one he insulted, gamble?"

"No. He was rich. And you just heard how uppish he was, at least according to a fellow who was lowish, who'd lost his ass at gambling and thought he was homesick for Russia when what he was really homesick for was a little luck, a little money, a little peace. But of course being who he was he wouldn't be able to let himself have a little luck, a little money, or a little peace. He'd be true to his writing, which was anxious and tortured and absolutely wonderful. He doesn't ever seem to have written a letter to anybody after having won a little and stopped. Maybe it never happened. He always stayed until he lost, so he could go on being Dostoevsky. It's funny it never occurred to him, though."

"I wish he'd had a lot of money," the woman said. "I know he was a good writer because we saw *Crime and Punishment*. Remember? We saw it before we were married. It was a very good movie. Everybody was so tortured. If he'd had a lot of money, would they have been?"

"He'd have gotten rid of the money. He would have *had* to. He thought he wanted living not to be a torture, but it wasn't so. It had to be a torture for him. It didn't mean anything otherwise. And it didn't have any beauty, either. That's one of the problems of writing. A healthy, happy, comfortable writer doesn't seem to have very much to write about."

"He could say, 'We was all having fun all the time,' couldn't he?"

"Yes, that's about what it would come to. And that's what's the matter with writing, with drama, with the human experience, even. Happiness doesn't seem to satisfy anybody. It doesn't seem to be exciting enough. People feel they're getting dull, losing their chance to live greatly. It's a lot of shit of course. I mean, it couldn't possibly be anything else unless we came right out and said that we hate being alive, that living is a swindle, that it's better to know pain and ugliness and trouble than to know pleasure and beauty and peace. But peace is the worst of all. Nobody knows what to do with it. It's not dramatic. It's not fun enough. It's not exercise enough for the soul. And so on. I don't get it. I think peace is dramatic, fun, and the best exercise for the soul, but there it is, nobody ever got it into a novel that was any good. It's a problem."

"Why do writers write in the first place? It seems such a problem all the time, and they all hate one another so, like Dostoevsky and Turgenev, and each of them always seems to believe what he believes so *positively*. What's there to believe so positively?"

"It's necessary for a writer to believe something or other

positively. He's as apt to be mistaken as not, but it's necessary. It's necessary for everybody else, too."

"I believe in money positively. And boys for girls and girls for boys. What do you believe in?"

"I believe in trying to find out what I believe in and why."

"What do you believe in without needing to know why?"

"You. Johnny, Rosey, the one coming, if he *is* coming. I gave it a lot of thought, though, and maybe I even know why I believe in these things positively without needing to know why, if you follow me. It's because as far as this life is concerned—and that's as far as I'm willing or able to go—there just can't be any argument against these things, and I don't mean these things at their best, either. I mean, these things the way they happen, the way they are, the way they must be, but I'm glad you're young and pretty and a good lay and that you have kids without losing your health and beauty and that the kids are healthy."

"I've never known you to be so sweet."

"I've told you these things from long before we were married. We've talked about them every time we've gone for a drive to a faraway city, and every time we've been alone this way and not just horny but trying to be people who care for one another and hope to understand one another enough to be helpful to one another when the time comes, as it sure as hell will and must, again and again."

"Aren't I helpful to you when the time comes?"

"No, and I'm not to you, either. I'd like to be and I try to be, but I know I'm not. Maybe it would be worse, though, if you were married to somebody else. Patience with people was never one of my strong points. I seem to know all I need to know about anybody as soon as I meet him. I've tried to be patient, but trying so hard is doing my health no good at all. I'm kind of jittery most of the time, and I've got several small muscles and nerves that have been bothering me quite a lot these past few years. They bother me most when I'm trying hardest to be patient. By nature I believe I'm addicted to fun, to health and pleasure and peace, and

121

to an intelligent attitude about intelligence, truth and personal growth, for it is fun to be intelligent, to know truth, and to grow. It *is* fun to try to be truly decent, it isn't torture."

"If we had a lot of money, things would be different," the woman said.

"A lot of money would help, but only for a start, not as an end. The money would be to pay the debts, so I wouldn't need to have them nagging at my thinking all the time. After that, I would have the most fun and best health it's possible for me to have."

"You ought to have a little more than just enough to pay the debts. Without money everybody gets tired. I know I do. Just knowing there isn't very much makes me tired. That's why I have to sleep so late in the morning, I think."

"Yes, you have to sleep late because you go to bed late and need a certain amount of sleep every night, but at the same time you don't get up earlier because you don't like your life."

"The debts aren't my fault."

"No. They're mine. I always gambled, but I never before had to think about the consequences if I lost. The result was I never lost much and frequently won. Now if I gamble I know it's not just me gambling, it's all of us, and if I lose it affects all of us. That puts apprehension into something that should be nothing if not unapprehensive. A gambler has got to be absolutely unapprehensive. He's just got to guess and not care very much whether or not he's guessed right. But the hell with it."

"I don't want you ever to gamble again," the woman said. "We've gone through hell. Promise?"

"Can you promise that you won't be miserable if you can't live as if I had an inexhaustible income? If you can, I can promise not to gamble."

"We can't live in this clerk's house forever, can we? I hate this house and always have and always will. I hate San Francisco. What good would it do to pretend that I don't? I hate the thought of waking up and still being in this lousy house in this lousy city."

"O.K. Doesn't that mean I've got to keep thinking of a way to get us somewhere that you like, in a house you like? Doesn't that mean I've got to be patient about everything every day, so patient that it's unhealthy? And doesn't that mean I can't sit down calmly and go about my work one day after another until I've got something written that doesn't make me sick to my stomach? And since this is so, don't I have to keep thinking of a quicker way of getting money than by writing, and doesn't this thinking always end in gambling?"

"Well, I can see you've got to put the blame on me again, the way you always do."

"No. Why don't you look at it this way? Put up with everything for a year. Know that after the year is over we'll be in a position to live a life more to your liking because during the year I will have worked and earned money and not had to think about how unhappy you are, *or* about gambling."

"I want to go to sleep, and I hope I'm not pregnant."

"I want to, too, and I hope you are."

CHAPTER
26

Much later, many sleepless moments later, long after many remarks of friendship, love, tenderness, animosity, hatred and loathing had gone unuttered one by one, and many kind or bitter questions had gone unasked, each of them listening to the breathing of the other, their hands almost touching accidentally now and then, each of them feeling the nearness and the ceaseless troubling of the other, the woman said, "Are you awake?"

"No, fast asleep."

"I'm scared."

"What about?"

"I don't know."

"If you mean you want to get in my bed, get in."

The woman scrambled naked and bouncing from her bed into his, backing up into him so that he could hold her the way he always did when she said she was scared.

"Isn't it all lies?" she said when she was snug and warm.

"I don't know."

"It must be. That's why all I believe in positively is money, and boys for girls. Money makes the lying boys do to girls and girls to boys so much nicer, so much easier to do."

"Lying's the beginning of everything wrong, deranging and dirty."

"Everybody does it, though. You know everybody does it. So if that's so, it must be necessary, too, and if it's necessary, isn't it better to accept it and let it go at that?"

"I don't know. Maybe it is. Even so, the idea doesn't appeal to me. I'll tell you why, too. It's impractical. It's so much simpler to start out by not lying. Why should anybody deceive anybody else? But most of all why should anybody deceive himself? The reason I hope you're pregnant is that if we have enough kids maybe one or two of them will be all right in this thing."

"The two we've *got* are all right in it, aren't they?"

"Who knows? Maybe they're all right until they're put to the test and then maybe they aren't all right. But if there are enough of them maybe one of them will be all right even after he's been put to the test."

"The test of growing up and becoming a shit like everybody else, is that what you mean?"

"Well, yes, it you want to put it delicately."

"Anybody will be a shit sooner or later. Anybody who doesn't die before he's eleven, at any rate. It's just that some people are bigger ones than others. And still others become shits without growing up first, like you, for instance."

The woman turned swiftly with delight to scramble all over the man, spilling laughter and pleasure all over him.

"What's so funny?"

"What I said. It's so true. I'm so surprised I said it. You are a shit and you never grew up. It's true. Ask anybody. You don't know your ass from a hole in the ground and yet you're always tring to figure out big things, trying to write them and get them straight. You were either born grown up and had to ungrow to become a shit, or you were a born shit and didn't need to grow up to be one, I don't know which."

"Very clever."

"All right. You love the truth. Try to tell me it isn't the truth."

"Only partly. Most of it's true, but what you've left out is that if it's true of me, it's much more true of others."

"That's just your lousy ego. Maybe it isn't much more true of others at all. How do we know? Maybe they don't even give it a thought."

"That's what I mean. If they gave it a thought, if they were willing or able to expose themselves to the risk of giving it a thought, they most certainly would come through in worse shape than I come through."

"Well, who's smartest, they or you? They are, and you know it. Why should they bother? Why should they go to all that trouble just to find out that they're shits?"

"Because it's progress," the man said. "Modern progress, like cigarettes an inch longer."

"Like *what* an inch longer?" She giggled and swarmed all over him again. "I wish you'd get thoughtful again. What's a cigarette factory? It's a penitentiary, isn't it? What's a million dollars? It's a curse, isn't it? What's holding up my curse?"

"Maybe it's a boy. Wouldn't you be glad if a boy was holding it up?"

"That's better. That's more like it. More thoughtful. I can just see the inside of your head—all broken bottles and rusty wheels and a few tired weeds trying to act like they're rose bushes, and you wandering around in there looking things over. I can just see you noticing something that looks like a blossom on a dried old weed and thinking to yourself, 'By God, here comes a true thing, a new thing, at last. Here comes beauty at last. Maybe it's going to be something perfect, whatever it is.' "

"The inside of my head is an old city on the banks of the Euphrates, and the things growing there are not weeds but olive trees and grapevines. I've seen the place many times in my sleep, and I've always felt at home there. It's a deserted place mainly but it is still magnificent, although in ruins."

"That's more like it. That small talk about cigarettes an inch longer was no good at all. What a liar."

126

"You don't believe I've seen the place?"

"You're inventing it right now. You saw a photograph of an excavated grocery store in your ancient-history book one day and that night you saw the photograph again in your sleep, and ever since you think you're a fine boy with fine dreams and a fine past."

"Do you know that's how it might have started at that? It *is* true, though, that I have been to ancient cities in my sleep. I remember hanging around a deserted building that was beside the sea once. That was a handsome dream if I ever had one. It was an abandoned place."

"What happened to the place on the banks of the Euphrates?"

"I may have invented that one. Or at any rate I think I went out of my way to put it on the banks of the Euphrates because that's where my people lived a long time."

"You and your people. You'd think they'd done something. Did they invent anything at all? Didn't everybody have to wait for a poor boy who got his ears boxed to invent the electric light bulb and the phonograph and everything else? I read all about it at school. One man, hardly belonging to *any* people, did all that inventing. What the hell did your people ever invent?"

"They say my great-grandfather Red Haig built fine-looking houses out of stone."

"Was that his real name?"

"It was."

"How did he ever get a name like that?"

"He had red hair."

"He didn't."

"He did."

"I thought they all had black hair in that part of the world."

"Most of them did. *He* had red hair, so his name became *Red*."

"Your hair isn't red."

127

"No, but yours is, and maybe Johnny's will be. The red helped, you know."

"Helped what?"

"Helped me decide you might just be the one."

"Which one?"

"To get in my bed and talk all night and be Johnny's mother."

"You thought about things like that?"

"You know damn well I did. We talked about things like that every time we were together. What's the matter? Memory gone blank?"

"Oh, I just thought that that was to string me along, make me feel better, make it a better lay, and all like that. I never took any of it seriously. Suppose I *didn't* have red hair, what then?"

"I may not have decided you might be the one."

"I could have been dyeing my hair red. How do you know I wasn't? It's easy to do. How do you know I don't have it dyed every time I go to the beauty parlor? Maybe my hair's black, for all you know. You may have got took."

"I just felt that the mother of my kids should have red hair."

The woman turned swiftly, swarming and slipping under him.

"It's all right," she said. "I don't want you to stop being thoughtful, but as for me, this is when I just let go and speak without thinking."

CHAPTER
27

"Is there anything in this apartment to eat?" the woman said.

"Not unless Marta put something in the refrigerator."

"Did you ask her to?"

"No, but maybe she did anyway. If she didn't, though, you could sneak downstairs and bring something up."

"Are you hungry, too?"

"I could go for a little something."

"How come? It's after three, you know."

"So what? Marta's downstairs. I don't have to get up tomorrow. I plan to sleep until evening."

"We can't do that. What about Lucretia?"

"You get up around two or three if you want to. Take a taxi and spend some time with her, and around seven take a taxi and come home and we'll go to dinner someplace."

"What about Alice and Oscar?"

"Bring them along. Bring Lucretia, too. What I mean is, I want to sleep until I'm sick and tired of sleeping. I need a lot of sleep."

"No, you've got to get up at a reasonable hour and take me in. It wouldn't do for you to fall out at this stage of the game. Things are going to be getting more and more exciting for Lucretia and I know she'd be miserable if you weren't there to notice how exciting and beautiful she is even with a funeral staring her in the face."

"I'd like to get out of it. After all, I never knew him. Why don't you just go in and then come back alone and we'll drive somewhere and have a good dinner? The funeral's not until day after tomorrow. I'll go to that funeral if you think I must, but for God's sake after the funeral don't bring her here."

"I've already asked her, and she's accepted. We can't get out of it now."

"Of course we can. Just *get* us out of it. The kids are sick or I'm sick, but get us out of it. I'll tell you why. I want us to spend four or five days together alone. There's a lot of things to talk about and we never get a chance to talk about them when we're taking care of the kids because we're always so tired and irritable. I'm not going to be trying to work, either. I just want to spend four or five days alone with you. It's very important."

"We can do it after Lucretia leaves. I told her to stay as long as she likes, but she won't stay more than a week."

"A week's too long. One night might be all right, but you can't get anybody to stay only one night. Just get out of it."

"What do you want to talk about?"

"Everything."

"Talk about it now."

"No. We started to have another fight tonight, and then we didn't. I think if we work on that a little more, we can get things in order. We need time, though, away from the kids and everybody else. I'll tell you something. I was going to tell you after things quieted down a little, but I'll tell you now. I've got more than six thousand dollars. It isn't enough but it's a lot. It's more than some people earn in a whole year of hard work. I won it on the horses. Two bets. Yesterday while you were at the beauty parlor and today while I took a nap at Lucretia's. You know my credit's good, so I took a chance. The first three bets yesterday ran out, but the next

130

one came in and I had a profit. I only bet one today and it came in, too, and paid more than twice as much as I had expected it to pay. Well, what I want to talk about is this. It's no good. I can't expect to do it again, but we've got *this* money and it'll keep us nicely for a year. I mean, I worried all the time, and I've got no business betting if I'm going to worry. I didn't worry for a while last night when I drove to the airport to get Alice and Oscar, but that was because I was drunk and desperate. All we had in the bank was a hundred and forty dollars and with Lucretia coming to town I knew that wouldn't last long, so I did what I did. But I know I was too lucky and I don't want to kid around any more and lose what I've got, and more that I haven't got, and then have to borrow, or try to, and make a fool of myself and a shambles of this family. I'm still pleased, because it *is* a lot of money and I got it on my nerve. I want to forget all about money now. I want to put the money in the bank and write checks as bills come in and forget all about money and think about this family and my work. I know we'll be all right in a year, maybe less. I'm very tired. I'm even scared because the money came so easily. It seems so simple. Just pick a horse and bet on him. But it's *not* simple. It's a miracle every time you win. I'm not up to miracles any more, and I'm not up to losing any more, either. I don't want to need to try to kid myself. I want to quiet down and forget money. Gambling owes me a lot of money, a lot more than six thousand, but I've got to forget that it owes me anything. I've got to be satisfied that I've gotten six thousand when I need it so badly, when all of us do. There's money coming from England all right. A hundred dollars or so. That's all. There's no other money coming. I haven't written a story in years that any magazine would care to buy. When I get back to work I may be able to write one every now and then and sell it. *While* I'm working on something long, I mean. You've got to help me, though. I don't mean just to *say* you will. You always say you will, and I know you try, but this time you've got to really

131

help me. You've got to put yourself out, otherwise there's no telling what's liable to happen to us."

"I *thought* something funny was going on." The woman laughed.

"Now wait a minute. Let's not be glad about this. It's disgraceful. It's pathetic. It's something to accept quickly and forget. It's something humiliating that nobody but you and I know about. It scares me, as if I'd won *sixty* thousand dollars. It might have been sixty, at that, I mean. It's absurd. It's ridiculous. I used to bet two *thousand* across the board, *all the time.* Well, I won this money betting two hundred across. Suppose when I'd telephoned I'd just said two thousand across from force of habit instead of two hundred? Leo would have taken the bet as quickly as he took the bet for two hundred. It's all the same, except that I might have won ten times as much, and I don't want to be bothered about it any more. I want to put the six thousand in the bank and see if you and I can get along and be decent human beings."

"If only you'd said two thousand," the woman said.

"Of course I should have said two thousand, but I didn't because I was scared to death. It would have been just as much trouble trying to borrow six thousand as to borrow six hundred, and you know what it does to me to try to borrow—from anybody. I wasn't going to tell you for a while. I thought I'd just keep up with you and Lucretia and Leander and Oscar and Alice and every now and then glance at the entries and phone a bet and maybe after a few days have thirty, forty, fifty, or sixty thousand dollars, but you know it's fantasy, it's murderous fantasy, it makes a fool of a man. Sure I should have said two thousand, but if that horse had run out of the money, who's to say I wouldn't have picked another and bet him two thousand, too, and if that one had run out of the money, too, who's to say, drinking all the time, knowing I'd know the outcome in the next fifteen minutes, I wouldn't have picked another horse and bet him two thousand, too? And who's to say that that horse wouldn't have run out of the money, too? And there I'd be. I'd have eighteen thousand dollars to pay in the morning, or at the latest the day after. Well, I don't want to think about it any more. I want to think about other things. I want to eat half a dozen scrambled eggs and go to bed and forget all about it. And you've got to help me. Do you understand?"

"O.K.," the woman said.

She got out of bed and put something on and went to the kitchen. There was nothing in the refrigerator, so she said, "Let's both go down and have a look at the kids while we're there."

They had a look at the kids, the woman said a few words to Marta, and then they took up everything they wanted. The woman made an omelet of eight eggs and some herbs, and they sat down and ate the eggs with toast and coffee and crisp bacon.

Then the man went to his bed and went to sleep, but it was all horses and money, winning and losing, and in his sleep that part of his mind which never slept said, "Forget it, for the love of God." But he couldn't forget it. Rosey crying the way her mother cried wouldn't let him forget it, Johnny flinging himself at him because he had beat Johnny's mother wouldn't let him forget it, the woman screaming wouldn't let him forget it, and he said to himself, "Pray to God, tell Him to forget it, turn it over to God, He can forget anything, turn it over to Him, let Him have it, let Him have all of it."

Then, at last he seemed to forget it, for he was in an old place, maybe it was near the Euphrates, and Johnny was glad there and Rosey moved about in the light there and the woman came to him there and did not bawl and she said, "I love our life, I love it because it's the life everybody's forever wanting to live forever and we're living it forever right now." His heart rejoiced, then, and he rested.

CHAPTER
28

He slept, dreaming of good things out of which to make good things, of the making of them, of talk, between a man and his woman, of loving anger between them, of chivalry between a man and his son, the son chivalrous and forgiving, of tenderness between a man and his daughter.

When he awoke, he awoke slowly and peacefully, believing it must be evening, but it was only six in the morning. He had slept two hours. He got out of bed to wander around the house, but his leg, now that he had relaxed at last, was gimpy again.

If he stayed keyed up one leg or the other went gimpy. If he relaxed, the same thing happened. He was getting old, that's all. Thirty-nine was a number of years at that, but the gimp had entered his body when he had been only thirty. It had startled him then, for he had not been prepared to acknowledge that he was getting old. He had not believed it was possible for him not to be tireless if he chose to be and he had always chosen to be. The pain was past anything he had ever imagined he might know: and it was all the more amazing in that there was no accounting for it.

He lifted his chair from the worktable in the living room and placed it at the window. He sat there and looked out at the street and the sky. It was a depressing place all right: all fog, all gray, all moist and cold. But where could you go? New York stank, too. There was something the matter with every place, but people lived everywhere just the same. The place didn't matter. The outskirts of Dublin might be a good place to go for a year or two. Oslo seemed like a pretty good place to stay in for a while. But a lot of people in Dublin and Oslo probably believed it would be fine if they could move to San Francisco.

He was relaxed now. He could think clearly. Two hours of deep sleep had simultaneously refreshed him and brought the gimp out of hiding, warning him to slow down. They'd find a nanny again. They'd take a long time about it and find a good one. She'd live in, downstairs, they'd live up. He'd work every day, slowly and easily, taking his time, without anxiety, without a schedule, without any thought of success or profit. He'd start work sometime between eight and ten and stop sometime between four and six. Then they would go for a long walk, or for a drive, or to dinner, or to the theater. They'd get to bed around midnight. They'd be relaxed, they'd get over thinking of living in terms of now, this instant. They'd take things easy and not ask so much of themselves. They'd get out of the hair of the kids, and get them out of their hair.

The buying of the house had always been right. It was two whole houses, each small, it was true, but still two separate houses, each with its own bath, kitchen, front door, and outside hall: each well furnished, carpeted, draped, easy to keep up. The gate at the entrance locked out the street any time they liked. It was a good house, a little like a ship pushing through fog, but a good house all the same, the sea not far off, to be seen from the back rooms and front. The sea gulls always flying around weren't so bad, either.

He couldn't imagine why they oughtn't to be able to live a good life in the house, why they had always wanted to get out of it. It was narrow, hugged on both sides by similar houses, and it was mainly up, had little depth, but everything

135

was there: the hall, the living room with the fireplace, the front bedroom, the kitchen with dining space, the back steps, the big basement for the car and storage. The back bedroom where the kids slept downstairs and the one where he was supposed to work but no longer did because it was too small. It was a fine house.

He heard the woman call out in the first stages of panic, "Darling? Where are you?"

"Here. I'm sitting at the window in the living room."

"Why? What's the matter?"

"Woke up."

"For God's sake, come to bed. I've been lying here awake, scared to death and listening to everything."

The man went to his bed and sat down.

"Well, can't you put something on? It's freezing cold."

"I don't feel cold."

"What's the matter? Why can't you sleep?"

"I slept beautifully, but then I woke up and wanted to walk around, only my leg's out of whack again, so I sat down at the window. What did you wake up for?"

"I always know when you're not in your bed. I feel it in my sleep. It scares me and I wake up. You were gone for more than a year, and there was always that empty bed beside me for so long. When you came back I guess I never got used to it. What's the matter?"

"I feel fine. I thought I'd be sleeping until evening, but there it is. I woke up."

"Aren't you going back to bed?"

"Not just yet. I always liked this hour. I used to get up at daybreak. Of course, it would be after sleep, not like this, but I still like this hour. Everything's new and clean and mournful but with a decent resignation about it, the resignation of a man who's got work to do and is on his way to it."

"Are you mournful?"

"I'm thinking about the impersonal *general* mournfulness. The quietude of the city at daybreak. Of course I'm mournful. So are you, so is Johnny, so is Rosey."

"I'm *not* mournful. I'm mad because you won't get us out of this awful house, that's all."

"Can't. Would if I could, but can't. But suppose I could, where could we go that wouldn't be *some* sort of a place with *some* sort of peculiarity of its own that would not appeal to us? Places are pretty much the same, and I think you ought to get it out of your head that this house is awful. It's not. It's a fine house. I looked at the whole thing a few minutes ago. People get the notion they've got to go somewhere when something else is the matter. Don't let anything be the matter any more. You'll enjoy life better."

"I wish it were that easy."

"Why not make it easy?"

"How?"

"Just notice the place with willing eyes. We've got two whole houses in one brand-new building, a fine yard, a big basement and garage, all paid for, two kitchens, two baths, two fireplaces, paintings by good painters hanging on the walls, books all over, a piano, an organ, radios, phonographs. It's in California, which is my home. It's in San Francisco, where I've lived the better part of my life. It's in a row of identical houses inhabited by retired Army officers of low rank, department-store clerks, bank tellers, and other people of that sort, but what's the difference? We've got money enough for a year. It *could* be a year of peace and work and fun, and now and then a drive to Reno for two or three days."

"I feel awful out here. I feel lonely and lost out here. I know that sounds silly because my husband's here, my kids are here, but it's so. I don't know why. Do you want to know what I've been dreaming? That we'd sold this house and gone to New York. Why couldn't we just do that? We could get a lot more for the house than we paid for it. We could sell it furnished, get rid of everything, go to New York, rent a new apartment, furnish it, start all over."

"Well, I don't want to go to New York, but let me think about it."

"We could do it."

"Let me think about it. I don't want you to feel lost and lonely."

"All *your* people are here. None of mine."

"We never see them. We've seen them only when you've insisted on it."

"Well, you hate my family and I hate yours, that's all."

"Yes, we do, but I've always worked best out here, and I think this is a better place for the kids than New York is, but let me think about it. I wish I didn't have to think about it, but let me think about it. I've just begun to feel relaxed, but I don't want you to feel lost and lonely. It isn't worth it. Nothing is."

"I don't mean right away. It would take a month or so to sell the place. It would take time to find a place in New York. Listen, it's half past nine in New York now. Shall I telephone that real-estate company we were in touch with when we lived in Long Island that winter?"

"O.K. See what they've got."

The man fetched the telephone with the long cord from the hall and handed it to the woman, who was soon speaking to the woman she dealt with in that real-estate company in New York. The woman talked a long time while the man wandered around the house.

"They've got some wonderful places," she said.

"How much are they?"

"Well, the least expensive one is ten thousand a year."

"That's too much. If we got twenty-five thousand for this house furnished, we'd have thirty-one thousand. The debts that have to be paid right away amount to around twenty thousand. That leaves eleven. By the time we are ready to go we will have spent at least a thousand or two but call it a thousand. That leaves ten. To furnish the new place on the installment plan would cost at least four or five thousand right away and at least five hundred a month for a couple of years. That leaves five thousand. The rent alone is almost a thousand a month. It's tiresome as all hell and I wish to

138

God it weren't, but what it comes to is that we've got to postpone moving for a while. In the meantime we've just got to make this place work. Do you agree that we would be making a mistake to try to move now?"

"I guess so," the woman said. "Damn those dirty high rents. Why can't they have wonderful apartments for fifty dollars a month?"

"What's the ten-thousand-a-year apartment *like?*"

"Well, to be perfectly honest, it's not much larger than just one of these flats. The rents are so high in New York. I wish I hadn't telephoned. What are we going to do?"

"I'm going back to sleep," the man said. "It makes me sleepy to think about it. I'm not going to ask you to like it out here any more because you can't."

He got back in his bed.

"I'm not going to ask you any more *to try* to like it. We'll get out of here. We'll go somewhere. If we can't go to New York, we'll go somewhere else that you like. Anywhere. You go back to sleep too. Forget all about it. We'll do it. We'll leave here as soon as possible."

The burden was home again, the anxiety was back, the tenseness, the deep troubling, all the things that nagged.

He was failing, that's all. He was no longer tireless, that's all. He was getting along and the gimp was in him forever now, to let him know. His carcass was fat now, his gut swollen, his neck thick. He was a bigger load than he ought to ask himself to carry, but he just couldn't get things back to form, back to the good old limits, back to resilience, ease and speed. He was slowed down, overloaded and wearing out. His face was puffy from eating more than he needed, and yet if he didn't eat so much he couldn't carry the load at all.

Well, he thought, there it is, that's all: old and fat and slow at a time when a man ought to be stepping out into his best vigor. Old, fat, slow and foolish. That's fine. The thing to do is sleep. Sleep on it. Sleep around it. Sleep through the day because the night got away. Sleep not to catch up, not to get back to sleep at night and work at day, not to get the order straight, but to forget for a few hours, to rest enough for a few hours in order not to fall into abject stupor. Sleep, not to be restored and refreshed and sent back to work, but to die awhile. Sleep, to die a little more, to let dying move in a little deeper, to add another layer to the fat, to make the slowness slower still, to push away a little farther the zest and decent resignation of the worker alive in a mournful world at daybreak, going to his work. Sleep, to escape life, to embrace death.

CHAPTER
29

He was up at twelve, and downstairs in time to see the kids before they went to their naps.

They were fine, full of games and stories about their adventures with Marta, and how Rosey climbed out of her crib and went out into the hall again and again, and how she kept Johnny awake and laughing half the night.

He picked the girl up, hugged her tight and walked into the living room with her, wanting her not to get up all night but not knowing how to tell her in a way that could be equal to the fun for her of doing it, or if it wasn't fun, equal to the need of it; for he knew that unless her mother and her father were in the house she would climb out of her crib and wander into the hall; and that even if they were in the house she would do it sometimes, but not nearly so much as she would with others, especially Marta, who loved her so much; and Negro girls and women who were always loving and knew about sitting in the dark and talking softly, or singing softly, to keep her from climbing out. He knew she had to climb and would if she believed she could get away with it. The new nannies fought it out with her, each in her own way, but they were fired if they spanked her (not because they spanked her but because they weren't interested enough

141

to figure out a better way of keeping her both at peace and happy). He had never been able to understand what she meant by climbing out of her crib, but she had begun to do it very early, long before most kids learn to climb at all, long before one had a right to feel that she was up to doing it safely; she often fell. He'd heard her fall. She got up, bawling the way her mother bawled, stunned, startled, frustrated, angry, and came out into the hall. And ten minutes later climbed out again and didn't fall. She meant something by it. She just didn't have to put herself to all that trouble for nothing. She just didn't have to leave a warm bed for a cold hall for nothing. But if she were wandering about searching for the scent of her mother, or the heat of her mother's body around her, or the sound of her mother's voice speaking to her with love, when she got these things she soon tired of them, she did not fall asleep in her mother's arms. She was just a little girl who had to climb out of her crib again and again, as long as she could get away with it, that's all.

He didn't scold her about it but pressed his face against hers and stood at the window of the living room. Then he turned her over to Marta, who washed her and undressed her. He sat in the kitchen chatting with the boy, answering a dozen or more questions about God, and then when Johnny and Rosey were in bed for their naps, he poured a cup of coffee for Marta and a cup for himself, and they sat and talked.

"She gets up," Marta said, "but I say *let* her get up. She wants to. No use taking that away from her. I don't mind."

"Can you imagine *why* she wants to?"

"No reason. She's a lively girl and very bright, just like her mother. She's exactly like her mother."

"Yes, she is, isn't she?"

"Exactly. I have never seen anything like it. So many kids I have seen, but none like their mother like this one. And that boy, he's a real brother to her. He puts up with her the way I've never seen a brother do."

"He hits her."

"Call that hitting? It's nothing. She's just like her mother,

142

and he's just like you. I watch them and listen to them and it makes me feel good. I just smile and laugh at everything, but those words, those dirty ones that they don't know are dirty. They say them so sweetly, so nicely, at just the right time."

"Can you stay a while?"

"As long as you like. I'm never happier than when I'm with those kids. Go away. Take your beautiful girl for a trip. You don't have to worry about anything. The gate is there. The phone is here. I'm an old Sunday-school teacher, and this is the greatest happiness for me."

"If there's anything you want, please let me know. I'll bring some ice cream. I know they like *that*."

"I *have* ice cream. We bought a quart on our walk yesterday afternoon. We're going for a walk this afternoon, too. I have my list. Everything's fine. Just forget all about the kids. Take your beautiful girl someplace nice and talk to her."

He went downstairs to the basement and had a look at the mail, but it was nothing. He drove to the bank and deposited the money. He drove to Ernie Perch's and asked Ernie to drive by the house and have a look at it from the outside, and to see what he might be able to get for it furnished. Ernie said he'd ask for twenty-seven fifty and would telephone only if he had somebody who would be apt to buy.

He bought an afternoon paper and turned to the entries. The eighth looked best: Like His Daddy, Nanby Pass, Brokers Sign, Sea Flyer, Adorable Torch, Shuffle Toe, Vain Doctor, Tia Juana, and Val Zun. Well, there it was. Like His Daddy, but he wouldn't bet. He wouldn't bet two dollars. He didn't want to. He couldn't. The horse would come in of course. It wouldn't pay much better than five to two, but it would come in. But let it. He wouldn't bet, that's all. And he didn't. (Later in the day he saw that Like His Daddy ran third to Nanby Pass and Sea Flyer.)

It should have won, he thought, especially since I didn't bet.

He drove home and went up and found the woman just opening her eyes.

"What time is it?"

"Two o'clock, that's all."

"Can I stay in bed a little longer?"

"You can stay as long as you like. The kids are fine. Marta says for me to take my beautiful girl for a long drive somewhere."

"Did she say that?"

"Those are her own words."

"She's a crook. She hates me."

"I don't think so."

"Well, I hate her. I can't stand the sight of her."

"Anyhow, they're fine, and we can do anything we like. But take your time because I've got some letters to answer anyhow."

"That damn Lucretia. Why hasn't she phoned yet?"

"Because she's still asleep. She'll be that way for days. Well, how about it?"

"Nothing yet," the woman said. "I guess I'm caught all right. I guess I'm stuck."

"Serves you right."

CHAPTER
30

The letters were difficult to write. They seemed irrelevant, purposeless and pathetic, as all writing had long since come to seem. It made him feel sick to go near the worktable.

What was there to say?

In letter, poem, story, or play?

It's tough. The going's tough. You'll never know the half of it. I'll never be able to tell the half of it. Somewhere along the line I was overwhelmed. I lost my luck. I'll never be able to tell the half of it. I'll never be able to get just a little of it straight. It doesn't want to come out straight. Living was always better than I ever knew how to tell; always more hideous than I ever knew how to tell. I lost it. I had to lose it. Everybody has to lose it. It's given only to be lost. I'll tell you what I wanted. Well, I don't think I can even tell you that straight. I guess I wanted plenty, but I can't tell it straight. What I wanted got tangled up in what I didn't want, and pretty soon I couldn't tell one from the other. I didn't want everything, but I wanted something like everything. I'll never know how to tell what I wanted. Well, there was the idea that all of it could be *received;* decently understood; decently accepted; but I can't tell it.

There was a letter from his lawyer saying an installment

on his income tax was due: almost two thousand dollars. He wrote out a check and sent it to the man and got that out of the way. That left less than four thousand.

There was a letter from a man in Oklahoma getting out a college textbook on the short story who wanted permission to reprint "The Man with the Red Nose," and a few words for college students to read about how he came to write the story.

"I was in San Antonio, Texas, one evening ten years ago," he wrote, "waiting for an automobile mechanic to find out why my car was getting overheated. I was waiting in the coffee shop across the street from the garage. A man came in and ordered coffee and two plain doughnuts. Two boys and two girls were at the far end of the place putting nickels into a jukebox and dancing. The waitress who had given me a cup of black coffee brought the man coffee and two plain doughnuts but the coffee had milk in it and the man said he was sorry, he had forgotten to say that he wanted black coffee and would she please let him have a cup black? The waitress said she would have to charge him for the first cup, and the man said it was all right. The man's nose wasn't red, it was no color at all. Nobody had a red nose in the place. I hadn't seen anybody with a red nose in years. Perhaps I had never seen anybody with a red nose, except a clown in a circus. I took a piece of paper out of my coat pocket and wrote on it: *Write a story called The Man with the Red Nose.* Three months later when I found the piece of paper among a lot of other pieces of paper, I sat down (I was in San Francisco) and wrote 'The Man with the Red Nose.' I have no idea why it wasn't 'The Man with the Black Nose.' "

Whatever it is, everybody has to lose it. Johnny had it and would lose it. Rosey had it and one day would find it gone. Would she cry? He hoped she wouldn't, but just thinking of Rosey finding it gone made him sick. He didn't want her to lose it. It was all right for Johnny to lose it, but just thinking of Rosey finding it gone made him angry. He didn't even know what it was.

146

The next letter was to his agent in London, who mentioned some offers from Italy, Sweden and Germany. They were poor offers and they would mean at most four or five hundred dollars in six months or a year, but he wrote and told the agent to accept the offers. There was no use telling him to try to improve the offers. Improve them for what?

The telephone bell rang, the woman answered it, and from her voice he knew it was Lucretia or Alice.

He answered a letter from a man in New York who said he had been a big producer in Vienna until Hitler got in there and that now he was producing in New York and would be honored to produce one of his plays. He told the man to telephone Maloney and talk things over with him. Then he wrote Maloney and told him to expect a call from the man and to hear him out even if it looked as if he had no money. Let the man from Vienna have *Free for All* if he wanted it.

Writing the letters irritated him. He stopped after the one to his agent because it was silly. He picked up the afternoon paper, sat on the sofa and had another look at the entries. Well, he'd have to give it another whirl, after all. What else? The two thousand tax installment was something he'd forgotten about. He'd bet two hundred across, win, get the two thousand back, or more, or lose six hundred.

"It was Lucretia," the woman said on her way to the bathroom. "Tell you all about it when I come back."

He dialed Leo and said, "Two hundred across on Family Circle in the sixth."

"Well," the woman said, "she's got a terrible hangover. Alice and Oscar want to go back this afternoon. Oscar says he's got a bad cold. Alice isn't talking to Oscar. She may not go back with him. After all, the kids aren't her own. They're only adopted. She wants kids of her own."

"What are you talking about?"

"Well, after we left last night the two of them got pissed and Lucretia told Alice she was going to marry a man who could get her pregnant, so why shouldn't Alice marry a man

147

like that, too? Of course Oscar doesn't know anything about this."

"She'll go back with him all right."

"Lucretia doesn't think so."

"O.K., what's the schedule?"

"I told her we'd be there in an hour."

"O.K."

CHAPTER
31

They found the retired villain and his young wife at the widow's, and he saw that hard times had come for the actor. Daisy and Alice began to speak loudly to one another about Lucretia (who was in the bath), so he began to speak to the actor, because the man needed help.

"Stay on," he said. "Don't fly back this afternoon. You won't have any fun to speak of here, but you won't have any at home, either. I mean, I hear you've got a bad cold. I've had a bad one most of my life. I'm sure you have, too. I mean, the hell with it. Alice hasn't got a bad cold. Make her happy."

"I feel something in my bones," the actor said. "I've been feeling jittery ever since I saw it happen. I wish I'd missed that. I've *acted* having an attack dozens of times and seen great actors act it, too, but it's not that way at all. It's not art, it's not acting. It's in the eyes, the damned light shoots out of them. It's like electrical flashes. But that isn't it, either. I mean, it's dying. It's getting it quick, and it's you, and you don't want to believe it. Do you know, he tried to brush it off even while it was happening because he was ashamed? He wanted to be alive, maybe young, and he was dying and wasn't young, and neither am I. Everybody's crazy about young tail. Well, there's mine over there with yours. You're not old but you're not young either, certainly not as young as your tail is, and hell, I'm so much older than mine, it's not funny, that's all. I love it. Who doesn't? But if you saw that poor phony—he must have been a phony all his life to try to brush it off the way he tried, he must have been a phony to be ashamed because his young tail with her fine young sex all over her was seeing him made a fool of that way—if you had seen him get his and then keep getting it, you'd feel a little older than you are, even. But I'm glad you didn't see it. I only wish to God he'd dropped dead before I ever got here because I've seen them dead and that's not so bad, but seeing them die, seeing that enemy take them, that's another story. I didn't sleep all night. I didn't mind being alone until five in the morning when Alice came by and took off her clothes and wanted fun. Wanted me to get her pregnant, she said. Right then. Get me pregnant, you old man, she said. What's the use not talking plainly? And sick as I was, drunk as she was, I wanted her, I forgot the phony dying and everything else and wanted her, wanted to make her pregnant, would have given anything in the world if I could, but there it is. She was young, drunk, and gorgeous, and I wanted all of it but couldn't have any of it. I mean, the poor body can't keep up with the mind, it fails, it's still there, it's still supposed to be alive, it's still supposed to have its vigor, but it doesn't, it's old, it's tired, and it's teased by the foolishness of the mind, it's teased by the eye, still looking, still wanting. I hope you don't mind my spilling all this. I'm troubled. She's not for me, that's all. I mean, I don't want to let her know I know. I don't want to let myself know, even. But she's not for me, just as Lucretia wasn't for that poor phony Leander. I know he couldn't really paint. He could flatter and get a lot of money for a phony portrait of a female monster, making her look like a fierce spirit, but he couldn't paint. Even I know he couldn't. But she's not for me. I'll be damned if I can pretend she is. I've buffaloed her into thinking she *is* for me or she's buffaloed

150

herself into thinking she is, but it's not so. I don't even think she's for one man at all, even the youngest, even the horniest, a man who lived for nothing else. He'd never be able to fill that hole. The more he tried the further away he'd be from succeeding. I'll stay on, though. Why not? I'm almost as much for her as any man could be. The kids love her, need her, and so do I, but what about what she needs? She *does* need it, too. She needs it, has a right to need it, has a right to try to see about working it out somehow. I thought money would get it all straight for me, but I've had more money than I know what to do with for more than thirty years. I need her— not Alice, if you know what I mean. I need *her*, and Alice has got her all over the place. She's her in good measure and the best I've ever known, but I don't need her as much as she needs him—a hell of a lot of him, more than I am, more than I could ever be, more than I've ever been. And there was a time not more than twenty years ago when I was a lot of him, almost enough. That's what's bothering me. But now I'll shut up, that's all, and we'll pretend I haven't said anything." The actor's eyes brightened, and then he laughed. "I'm not giving her up. If it kills me, I'm not. Let it kill me. Something's bound to, in any case, something *ought* to, let it be her. I want her, more and more of her, and I'm going to see about eating a little better today than I did yesterday. I've got to eat, that's all. Whatever's ahead, I want to have beans in me when the day's over and she's taking off her clothes, that's all. We're staying on. I'll tell her in a minute. It'll be like saying, 'O.K., Mama, I want more of you, I want it on your terms, I want it on any terms, and wait until tonight.' You watch what happens, and watch me ham it up a little, too. Look at her, for God's sake. Look at the both of them, talking over the big problem. Look at how serious they are about it. Well, watch how Oscar works on Mama."

The actor hadn't been wasting time even as he talked. He had been acting steadily, standing higher in his body, limbering up, stretching himself, tightening his muscles, lifting his head higher, reaching out with his hands to get the blood circulating a little better, pushing one leg out slowly and tensely, and then the other, and now, now that he was ready to give over, he was truly glad about it, it was certainly the thing to do, and if one were able to know, how would one know it weren't the wisest thing he could do? His eyes brightened, his face lost its hopelessness, its wretchedness, its bewilderment and fear and age. He looked young and equal to very nearly anything.

"Look here," he said with a very young voice, not moving but seeming to be in youthful movement. "Look here, Mama. It's twenty-four hours before the funeral. I say why not all of us drive out to a good restaurant someplace and have a hell of a lunch, then fly to Reno for some real wild fun, then stop for a while around three in the morning, sleep till noon, fly back, and bury the poor son of a bitch."

Well, the actor's wife knew it was coming. She had known it from the first two words he'd said. Her face came alive and she ran to him and said, "Oh, Oscar, are you really feeling better? No, I won't let you do it. We'll fly home this afternoon." And she hugged and kissed him. The actor glanced over at the man and winked. He was O.K. again. He loved it.

"Go in and tell the widow to shake her fat ass a little," the actor said. "Let's get going. This place would make anybody feel sick."

The actor's wife ran into the other room to see what was holding up Lucretia, and the woman went to the man and said, "I'm so glad you cheered Oscar up."

The actor went after his wife and the man said, "He cheered himself up."

"We're going, aren't we? We're going to fly to Reno with everybody, aren't we? For God's sake, you're not going to spoil things, are you? We owe it to poor Lucretia. She needs distraction. We'll have the nicest time. But why should we wait to eat? Why not eat in Reno?" She lifted her voice now so the actor would hear, "Why not eat in Reno, Oscar? Why not catch the next plane?"

"O.K.," the actor called back, "but while we're waiting for Lucretia to get ready, I'll have a thick steak—nothing else, so I can eat again in Reno."

"We'll go to that new hotel," the woman said. "I'll telephone them now. I want a suite overlooking the river. What's the name of that river? We can afford it, can't we?"

"Sure we can," the man said.

Phone calls were made for two steaks, for reservations on the next plane, for three suites one above the other at the new hotel, and then the man telephoned his home.

"Marta," he said, "we're going on a little trip. We'll be home tomorrow night. How are the kids?"

"They're just waking up," Marta said. "They're fine. You have a good time with your beautiful wife."

DATE DUE

DEMCO